PRAISE FOR
THE COMPLETE HISTORY OF NEW MEXICO:

"The stories here are very good, but the title novella brushes great-ness, getting as it does to the deepest layers of American myth. In 'The Complete History of New Mexico,' McIlvoy shatters form, col-lating social history, geography lesson, photo gallery, pseudo-memoir, insanity plea. The result is the most original, funniest, and most powerful work he has written."   **—David Shields**

"Kevin McIlvoy channels the hilarious, heart-rending voice of fifth-grader Charlemagne J. Belter to tell the history of New Mexico in ways no one but sweet Charlemagne himself could confabulate or imagine. This magical collection of tales soars with mysterious visions: a mother with a melted hand, a fiberglass rhino that fills a barn and yet floats free as if through a keyhole. Kevin McIlvoy delivers us into our greatest joys and darkest compassion to show us the tender place where cruelty and mercy converge between a nurse and a starving boy, a dying mother and her children, a pas-sionate student and the harsh teacher who finally, despite her fierce will, cannot resist him."   **—Melanie Rae Thon**

"Kevin McIlvoy's great gift is to take nothing for granted. *The Complete History of New Mexico* is a landscape where the familiar is made new and strange in ways that both disturb and satisfy. This is an original, and in the best possible sense, a subversive book. Wonderful stories, artfully told."   **—Jean Thompson**

"If you could distill the generous voice of Rick Bass, the verve of Lorrie Moore, and the exacting prose of Charles Baxter into a single concoction, you might have something close to Kevin McIlvoy's re-markable *The Complete History of New Mexico*. Kevin McIlvoy has long been one of this country's most talented and original writers, and with this book he has outdone himself."   **—Brady Udall**

"Kevin McIlvoy's *The Complete History of New Mexico* is a collection of ingeniously interlocking stories that pack a cumulative wallop. His New Mexico is full of places like bars called U Dam Right and full of people who feel like they've fallen out of one way of knowing without having figured out how they might live instead. They feel like they've been learning pulling apart while everyone else has been learning putting together. They often manage to torque the colloquial into the epigrammatic: 'If you say it out,' one tells us, 'what can happen happens.' Many of these stories—like 'Chain' and 'Been So Good to Me' and 'Permission'—deliver the extraordinary on every page, and all of them combine to create a heartening universe of believers glimpsed trying to peer into each other's bare awfulness, but even so seeking the wider net, the straighter path, each of them hoping to regain what is gone or summon what has not yet come."   **—Jim Shepherd**

"Kevin McIlvoy's book reads less like a collection of stories than a series of musical riffs, performed by those marginalized by youth, bad luck, or fanaticism. And why not? Who else should sing us the blues, if not McIlvoy's unlikely seers, all too aware of the importance of a refrain? Imp-like, a minor character in one McIlvoy piece pops up as the protagonist of another, and the title story—the collection's masterpiece—is a three-parter that develops over the course of the book. McIlvoy ingeniously uses nonfiction forms (the grade-school history paper, the chain letter), as well as more conventional structures, to open the reader to the book's real subject: the painful mysteries of love. It is a testimony to how humorously and movingly McIlvoy does this that one finishes a story thinking less 'Oh, that's sad' than 'Oh, play it again. Play it again.'"   **—Debra Spark**

The Complete History
of New Mexico

Other Books by Kevin McIlvoy

A Waltz
The Fifth Station
Little Peg
Hyssop

The Complete
History of
New Mexico

stories by

Kevin McIlvoy

Graywolf Press
Saint Paul, Minnesota

Publication of this volume is made possible in part by a grant provided by the Minnesota State Arts Board, through an appropriation by the Minnesota State Legislature; a grant from the Wells Fargo Foundation Minnesota; and a grant from the National Endowment for the Arts, which believes that a great nation deserves great art. Significant support has also been provided by the Bush Foundation; Target and Mervyn's with support from the Target Foundation; the McKnight Foundation; and other generous contributions from foundations, corporations, and individuals. To these organizations and individuals we offer our heartfelt thanks.

MINNESOTA
STATE ARTS BOARD

NATIONAL
ENDOWMENT
FOR THE ARTS

Stories in this collection were published, in different form, by
Chelsea, Harper's, Mid-American Review, The Missouri Review, Ploughshares, River City, The Southern Review, Tierra, and *TriQuarterly.*

"Cold Weather Blues" written by Muddy Waters © 1964, 1992
WATERTOONS (BMI) / Administered by BUG
All Rights Reserved. Used By Permission.

Published by Graywolf Press
2402 University Avenue, Suite 203
Saint Paul, Minnesota 55114
All rights reserved.

www.graywolfpress.org

Published in the United States of America
Printed in Canada

ISBN 1-55597-413-9

2 4 6 8 9 7 5 3 1
First Graywolf Printing, 2005

Library of Congress Control Number: 2004109264

Cover design: Julie Metz

Cover photograph: Kevin McIlvoy

In thanksgiving for the miracle of
Colin & Paddy McIlvoy,
the author offers these retablos.

CONTENTS

The Complete History
of New Mexico

Chain

Love crosses impossible distances for any man who says Yes, but stops on the very spot in the very hour that one man will not. How far will you travel and for what treasure? Leavers believe that Believers will leave.

On its way to you this miracle has traveled without rest seven years across seven continents to bring countless men the wildest dreams, the private wishes, pleasures and blessings of love they have never expressed ever.

This is not a test.

Copy this out. Copy this down to stop love's stubbornness, why don't you?

No strings are attached to your gift from the universe of believers, brothers and lovers, lovers and brothers, who want you to know the bliss they have known since sending out seven handwritten copies for seven other men within one week of receiving this correspondence.

A man looking for a liver for his dying daughter did not send The Letter. Five days later two donors matched but no doctors would put her on their lists. With critical time passing, two more donor matches were found but reassigned and, at the very end, the original two as well. She fell into a coma and would have died. She would have died. She would have. Another chain letter arrived in the mail on what would have been the last day of her life. The rest is one link in the legend of the long unbroken chain along which we reach hand over hand until our own hands are exchanged for the hands we need. Do you believe? The Receivers believe that Believers receive.

You and your lost friends, your lost lovers and you, can join hands again, can't you? You need a wider net, a straighter path, an unmarked, open, simple single map. To regain what has gone, to summon what has not come, to find what could not be found, Heaven sends a lever that fits your hand, and asks only that you copy down and pass on these seventeen-hundred words one man wrote in the allotted time long ago.

Why won't you roll away the one, white, flat stone in your way? Copy this down to know how you knew and will know innocence again: a giant's giant sleep, a mote's looping flight, a shadow chasing light on tree limbs, a child's hand—your hand—reaching in dreams for the seven faces of the moon. Copy this out. Copy this down.

After four years of searching, losing hope, and searching, three brothers in their seventies found their father seven states away—on the same day he sent seven copies of this letter to seven utter strangers.

Seven men in the same emergency room at 7 A.M. on a Saturday in July survived food poisoning because they sent The Letter, and didn't delay and didn't ask why and will never regret it now though they all admit it, they all admit it: how silly they felt and rude and ashamed. Can we comprehend it? The Survivors believe that Believers survive.

No chances were involved and no coincidence and no code names and no secret tricks and no risks of any kind in all these documented cases of joy in over seventy years of The Unbroken Chain.

When will it end?

Are you a deluded man deluded by other men into sharing delusions about when you must quit being children and must break words like black bread and must never make words particles of sand or cedar shavings you mill between your palms and spread across your hands or bring to your mouth or taste only to taste the sun or eat to eat the whole forests and oceans of rising and falling longing you have known? When will it end?

It will end when you copy this out to write one length of chain seven links long, and pass this task on and pass this task on and pass this task on so that when The Chain lengthens by seven times ten and ten times seventy again you are that many chain lengths closer to being loosened and unbound. Copy this down. Copy this hymn by a chorus of men who only wish to sing but who need a brief dusk, in the meantime, a long dawn, in the meantime, seven dreams of seven fortunes to reclaim what has come and gone, to find and lose and find what should be found.

A man who fell in love with the same woman seven times, who loved him less each time he fell, sent seven other falling, failing men The Letter. And in only seven years (which seems a long time if you are not that man), in only seven years (the smallest piece of a life's long chain) she wrote him to say that someday she would write to him again.

If you are not that man that much doesn't mean much. But seven ifs can become seven whens if you are him. Are you him?

Heaven sends scissors that fit your hand, and demands you use them to cut Doubt. Cut it down, spit it out like laughter underwater. Face it the way you face your cord being cut, or the jump that begins your flight, or the first silence that announces your deafness, or the distance and dearness and the blame and forgiveness sounding all at once in her voice, or the loss of breath, and the next, and the next, last loss, or her closeness that even in remembrance feels like wondrous blindness.

When will you write the lines of this one letter to trace out the face of the wind on the water you drown in?

A teacher, too proud of his wit, too ready to punish all Lovers with it, who made fun of The Letter in a high school class fell ill that instant before his students. In a fever, and growing hysterical, he passed out, and he felt or thought he imagined he felt fourteen young men's arms lift him up like a tablet, and seven hands write upon his skin with the spilling ink of words that were black twine, ragchain, and kitewing flying him beyond his classroom and higher into his dreams, if they were dreams, where his tongue stalled, melted, dissolved, and tumbled like hail from his mouth, and where his doubt wilted and his wide desk widened and on it were the seven copies he would send when he awakened.

Can you name seven young men who never made a wish? And

seven old who never will again? And seven old and seven young who failed to write to the women and men who loved them? Can you name seven who don't also know seven once-wishing, would-be-wishing or will-be-wishing will-be-writing would-be-writing writing men? Name them.

In the long run, to be a Lover you need new hope in unlikely luck, an accidental bonus, improbable justice, one letter in one envelope with which you can address your lack of conviction seven times over, don't you?

To be a Lover, to be a Lover, Heaven, in the long run, makes you poorer by the power of seven and offers you one nothing less than nothing and asks something of you seven times more than you have ever done.

You might never in your lifetime receive another letter like this one. Begin writing.

THE COMPLETE HISTORY OF NEW MEXICO

PART I

Mr. Belter:

Your bibliography is incorrect. Where are your footnotes? Your outline is insufficient. Certain quoted passages are much too long.
   MINUS 20 points.

What is the meaning of your illustration? Where are your assigned illustrations? The colored map of New Mexico is especially important.
   MINUS 10 points.

Did you use a dictionary? I don't think so. Historical places are not "found." They are "founded." Beaver are not "tramped." They are "trapped." The word is "omNiscient" not "omiscient." Do you understand comma usage? Does your stepmother understand?
   MINUS 12 points.

The Navajos held captive at Bosque Redondo were not tortured. The cattle boom did not end because the cattle had an uprising. New Mexico did become a state in 1912. Did you not learn these facts? Did you make up lies?
   MINUS 50 points.

Why did you never discuss the Jornada del Muerte?
   MINUS 5 points.

I want to see your father and your stepmother immediately.

3 of 100 points = F

Mrs. D. Bettersen

The Complete History of New Mexico

by Charlemagne J. Belter

Mrs. Dorothy Bettersen
Fifth Grade
November 27 1964

MY OUTLINE

The Introduction
    A) The theme of Don Juan Onate and the Jornada Del Muerto
    B) Sandia Man and Folsom Man
    C) Our dads

I.   Santa Fe Found
    A) Omiscient facts
        1) Mrs. Orofolo
        2) Bus
        3) Mr. Alvarezo
        4) Awful
    B) Indians
    C) Spaniards
        1) The Spaniard letter
        2) Santa Fe

II. Albuquerque Found
    A) Franciscans
        1) bells
        2) books
        3) ropes
    B) Pueblos Rebel
    C) De Vargas Returns
    D) A Pueblo Nightmare
    E) Jornada Del Muerto

III. War With Mexico
- A) Colonizing
- B) A long voyage
  - 1) William Becknell
  - 2) The Santa Fe Trail
- C) Mr. Alvarezo's orchard
- D) Beaver Boom
- E) Some Texans try something
- F) More of Mr. Alvarezo and my illustration: Bus's Bus Route

IV. New Mexico Mined
- A) President Polk declares
- B) Mrs. Orofolo
  - 1) Chile field
  - 2) A tree in a fence
- C) A Gadsen Purchase
- D) Beaver Hats
  - 1) Buffalo
  - 2) More about Pueblos
  - 3) Conquistador Women
- E) Mrs. Orofolo at her table
  - 1) The Seven Cities
  - 2) The Arizona Territory
  - 3) The Goodnight-Loving Trail
- F) Bosque Redondo
  - 1) Mines Boom
  - 2) Daniel decides
  - 3) Geronimo

V. My Conclusion
- A) Statehood
- B) Good-byes
- C) Plans to leave for Orla

THE COMPLETE HISTORY OF NEW MEXICO

My Introduction

I am going to write about the state of New Mexico and put in some maps and stuff from the encyclopedia. My theme is the Don Juan Onate trail and the Jornada Del Muerto. But I might write some other important things which as it turns out my stepmother got angry about and said she wouldn't type this until my dad said "Dammit now it is history" and told her maybe there weren't commas in those days.

All of it was way before we decided to move to Texas and then not move there. It goes like this.

My dad and me moved from Arizona which was in 1963 to a town that's hardly a town. Hatch. It's close to nothing but it's on Highway 185 where one time anyway a lot happened on the Onate Trail. Sandia man and Folsom man were around. It was about 15000 years before the highway was made but they were good hunters so they did okay. I had a new friend Daniel who also came from another school somewhere to here.

Daniel's dad was older but he was my dad's friend. Neither guy was married. They even both smoked cigarettes. We were nine and we thought that was the neatest thing ever to know that. Man oh man. Almost all the same.

My dad was a Small Repairs Man and his dad was a Writer which we thought was also neat because his dad used typewriters and my dad repaired them and other stuff with moving parts that stopped moving right. It was funny sometimes too. Daniel always had a headful of new words.

Santa Fe Found

"Chum. I'm omiscient" Daniel said to me one afternoon around June on our bikes. "I'm plenty omiscient."

"So?" I said. If you need to know I got that name Chum because my name is Charlemagne which is goofy.

"So I can know about everything" Daniel said.

And when I made him tell me like what he said like he knew that Mrs. Orofolo had a third arm growing out of her back and Bus the Greyhound bus driver was a topsecret double FBIA agent. And he knew a lot more like how Awful—Mr. Alvarezo's dog—had tattoos on his forelegs that said USMC and LSMFT.

It had to be true.

Mrs. Orofolo who I guess had been a Mrs. once but wasn't anymore really had a big lump on her back like a third shoulder. Bus who called himself Semi was a guy who never said anything not good morning or anything and nobody knew his real name so he was named Bus after the Greyhound superbus he drove like a bat outta hell up and down the Highway. I never saw no tattoos on Awful but I never knew nobody who got close enough to look because the talk was that Awful killed other dogs and fed them to Mr. Alvarezo's pigs who were supposed to be big and bloated and maybe could of had tattoos you never knew.

The Anasazi had tattoos all over everywhere and they drew all kinds of weird things in the Chaco Canyon. Then the Pueblo Indians were around about 700 years ago. There was a lot of them in those days.

Then this guy from Spain came and gave them a big long letter they couldn't read if their life depended on it which it did. The end of it went like this.

> Wherefore, as best you can, I entreat and require
> you to understand this well which I have told you, tak-
> ing the time for it that is just you should, to compre-
> hend and reflect, and that you recognize the Church as
> Mistress and Superior of the Universe, and the High

Pontiff, called Papa, in its name, the Queen and King,
our masters in their place as Lords, Superiors and
Sovereigns of these islands and the main by virtue of
these gifts, and you consent and give opportunity that
these fathers and religious men, declare and preach
to you as stated. If you shall do so you will do well in
what you are held and obliged; and their Majesties,
and I, in their royal name, will receive you with love
and charity, relinquishing in freedom your women,
children, and estates, without service, that with them
and yourselves you may do with perfect liberty all you
wish and may deem well. You shall not be required to
become Christians, except, when informed of the truth,
you desire to be converted to our Holy Catholic Faith,
as nearly all the inhabitants of the other islands have
done, and when his Highness will confer on you numer-
ous privileges and instruction, with many favors.

If you do not do this, and of malice be dilatory, I
protest to you, that, with the help of Our Lord, I will
enter with force, making war upon you, from all directions, and in every manner that I may be able, when
I will subject you to obedience to the Church and the
yoke of their Majesties; and I will take the persons
of yourselves, your wives and your children, to make
slaves, sell and dispose of you, as their Majesties shall
think fit, and I will take your goods, doing you all the
evil and injury that I may be able, as to vassals who do
not obey but reject their master, resist and deny him;
and I declare to you that the deaths and damages that
arise therefrom, will be your fault and not that of his
Majesty, nor mine, nor of these cavaliers who came
with me.[1]

"Daniel" I said. "How do you get omiscient?"
He had platter eyes and a burr haircut grew real fast over and
behind his ears so he was pandafaced all the time which I didn't

much remember until I just now wrote it. I just knew him about seven months. He said his dad said you can't get certified omiscient. It comes and goes. "It comes and goes" he said and I didn't like the way he said it because he got a terrible kinda Indian Mask look on his face.

"Daniel?"

"Don't know. It only happens."

He was my real buddy and wouldn't keep it from me if he knew how to make me omiscient so I said "Don't it beat all get out."

"Don't it" he said. It must've been about June. We both watched an onion truck come over a hill on the highway and into town. If you ever smelled a fresh scab that's what an onion truck smells like. It could be a good smell even.

"He's going to call me home" Daniel said.

And sure as heck he did.

And then Coronado who was Spanish explored around. Pretty soon he found Santa Fe in 1610.

Albuquerque Found

The Franciscan preachers who liked to build churches built them everywhere they wanted. They hauled all the stuff with mules or with slaves. They liked trees and planted them all over. The Pueblo Indians some of them anyway didn't like the big churches or their loud bells or thick books or maybe they didn't like the look of those ropes around the Franciscans' middles.

My bed was way too low to the ground. If I dangled my arm over I could touch my elbow to the floor. Our house wasn't big or nothing. Our toilet was an outside job. So I watched the Untouchables with Dad and because we didn't make popcorn we had a fight.

"It's bad for you to have it all the time" he said.

"Prove it" I said.

He called me a smartaleck and told me to shut my trap. So I did. But I was hungry was the thing. Before bed he made me some jelly on crackers and sat on the floor by my bed and kind of looked at himself. Then he said "Chumbuddy. You know I was joshing about you shutting your trap."

I asked for another cracker.

He broke it into four squares and put extra thick jelly on every one. "What do you say? Truce?"

I didn't tell him about the Pueblos going crazy and rebelling. I said "I knew you weren't mad or nothing."

"Good." His jaw locked up grinding some big thought between his teeth I guess.

So the Spanish Conquerors went away. It took them almost ten years to get up the guts to come back. Then they came back mad. A lot of them. Their main guy was named De Vargas which is Spaniard for "From the Vargas."[2]

I could see him after the lights were off laying in his bed pretending he wasn't looking at me. That and the crackers must have gripped my guts because I had a nightmare.

I was in the back of the bus which was long as the long hall in school. And we were going maybe two or three hundred miles an hour and Mr. Alvarezo's pigs had the window seats but weren't

17

looking out the windows. All their heads pointed one way. The wind whipping through their gums under their snouts making a noise like you never heard. Like toilets upchucking. Bus was pulling the handle to the bus door and sucking it open and closed. He wore a conquistador helmet. He was saying something to Daniel who was sitting way up at the front. Daniel was lit up every time the door opened. He was buswindow green when it shut. His head shook no to Bus and his shoulders quivered kind of. And I called him. "Daniel. Hey!" But all the pigs' heads turned towards me and the wind through their stubby hairs made a crackling sound like little fires. "Hey" I said and didn't say no more. The door sucked open and Bus pulled the handle and sucked it closed and I thought No Daniel. Daniel! Bus sucked the door open. The whole long everything blew full of onion skins and they whirled and stormed and met in a million little seams. And there was Mr. Alvarezo in a long brown robe with a white rope around him. He took Daniel by the shoulders. He said "Joe said. Joe said. Joe said." And I thought Daniel! Hey! but the pigs' necks all creaked when they nodded up and down "Joe said. Joe said. Joe said." Up and down. At the front of the bus Mrs. Orofolo was staring right at me. The arm on her back was holding the driver's wheel. In her other two arms she was ringing a big silver bell and showing her gums which were pig's gums.

My dad woke me up. He looked at me funny but said "Good morning" and didn't make no big deal about me shouting "Joe said. Joe said" and all before I really came awake.

I guess to the rest of the old world it was no big deal. The Spanish conquered it all back the whole state which wasn't even a territory in those days. In fourteen years or so the Pueblos were bored or sore or sick. They said "Okay already."

We ate oatmeal. I make my own toast most times. But he made me toast that time. He sat real far apart from me. "Is everything all right with Daniel?" he asked me.

"What do you mean?"

"Nothing."

It was 1706.

War With Mexico

One morning Daniel said to me "I'm adventuring. It's the first day." It was Sunday so not too many things had happened. They had found Albuquerque. They had built some villages posts grave-yards and such. It was already July and hot but Daniel had a jacket on that he wore or his sister Marty wore. They traded off.

"Adventuring" I said.

He looked like he was thinking about it. "A way down the road I'm going lad."

"Lad?" I wondered what book he was reading. You never knew.

Daniel must have jumped out of bed right through his front door in one jump is all I can say because every morning his face always had pillow wrinkles on it. His hair was half of it straight up and half of it there in the front smashed down which could make him look like a roadrunner because he had a quick neck and head.

"A long voyage Chum my lad. I'll take me one Miner Character."

"Me?"

"I'll be Major. You have to have a Miner and a Major."

It sounded good. "Me then I guess."

"A whole bunch of things have to happen to me lad. I shall have to get sick or die. Or change a real lot. Maybe all of it."

I was catching on. "And I shall?"

"Be Miner." He pointed to the road. "It's an adventure" he said because I guess he liked that word. But he knew it didn't prove nothing. "You. Shall." There's a word makes your front teeth feel all noble. "You shall get me into trouble. You could get me out of it sometimes too."

That was in 1821 when William Becknell was tracking wagons over everyplace. He flattened a lot of cactus and stuff and had short legs in a picture of him and a big chest. It was the Santa Fe Trail. The Great Plains were "great"[3] is how people put it. Daniel said Mr. Alvarezo lived only "eight leagues off" and "was trapped by Sircomestands" which meant to me he was about as far away as eight baseball fields and surrounded by pigs in armor probably. We'd never been to his house because of Awful.

19

"We shouldn't" I said when we got to the high brick wall back by Mr. Alvarezo's garden.

"We SHALL" said Daniel. His mind was all made up. He said the word like it was in capitals and triple underlined but my stepmother will not triple underline anything.

I could be talked into it just by that word SHALL if you can believe it.

On the other side of the wall was the New World.

Mr. Alvarezo didn't have pigs. He had an orchard. He had a whole acre backyard of orchard with trees you never seen and some pecans and plums and peach and fig and apple trees and not one pig in sight.

Up the center of the orchard was a lane which had maybe thirty rose bushes on either side and went straight to his backdoor. All the roses were pink.

I followed Daniel into the orchard. "Man oh man."

"Wondrous" he said.

This History guy Castenada wrote it down. "The ground they were standing on trembled like a sheet of paper." Pedro was his first name.[4]

"Daniel we could eat couldn't we?"

The idea didn't fit him right. He squirmed in it. "Your dad know Mr. Alvarezo?"

"No. Yours?"

"Nope."

We sat under a fat pecan and ate some plums. Some overripe peaches too. That was early and lots of weird things were going on. Like pelts were invented and beavers were being tramped in the Rockies. It was a Boom. More women came West. "Have some more peaches" I said. The Texans wanted all of Mexico. They still do is my bet. In 1841 they tried to take it and it didn't work. "Here" I said.

"Can't."

"Plums are good."

"Shhh" Daniel said and we flopped onto our stomachs quick because Mr. Alvarezo's back door had slammed. Awful must've been

20

behind it. Over and over he barked three barks at a time like he was barking Let me out! Let me out! Let me out!

And it was Mr. Alvarezo alright. You could tell because he had greasy black long hair and a black greasy beard which didn't look like a beard much. It looked like a mess he got all over his face and neck eating black licorice. His black eyes were real small and far back inside his sockets with only a little white around them like they were rocks blocking light out. He was skinnier than most of his trees.

Anybody could walk up that row of rose bushes and look like His Majesty The King of Spain. Mr. Alvarezo looked junky. He had a dirty cardboard box in his one hand and big scissors in the other. He set down the cardboard box at the rose bush four or five feet high near the wall. I was laying on top of my left arm and I wanted to move but he was real close.

Daniel had flopped down right next to me and I could smell his sweat and the fruit sap and rose scent all at once which smelled like bad news. When Mr. Alvarezo put down his box and scissors and started talking to the rose I felt my heart jump where my pinned arm crossed it. And the arm felt like a giant root I'd never be able to tear up quick enough to run.

Mr. Alvarezo bent a rose to him then moved his hand down and rested his skinny dark arm along the cane. He was saying things. Every other word was Therese and Therese. Like how if you ever heard old Catholic priests saying things they say them over and over? You should meet my stepmother who is Catholic—and how.

He was saying "Therese. Remarkable Child. Therese. The Holy Face. Therese. The Perfect Gift." And all the time he was closedeyed and creeping his greasy fingers through each petal of this one small pink rose. "Therese. Showering Faith. Therese. Burning with Zeal." My hand was buzzing some. I really needed to move. Mr. Alvarezo's hand kind of shivered on the rose. Daniel was breathing like he was not all right. I thought it couldn't go on but I didn't know about Catholics then like I do now.

Mr. Alvarezo moved his whole bony self more into the rose bush. He touched along the rosy edges of the petals in the center. "Therese.

Inflamed Spirit. Therese. Passionate Mirror. Gentle Temple. Warm
Fountain." He put his first two fingers deep inside the center of the
rose. He touched the petals and his own fingers with his closed lips.
He was softer and softer saying things right into the rose real slow
and some of it in Spaniard. I couldn't get any of it after that.

It was maybe noon. The tree shadows backed themselves back
up into the trees. And Daniel kind of bunched into his jacket so
he looked like he was doing the same. All the dark shadows under
his head went up into his face. He put his head down with his face
smack into the ground.

It went on and on. Then Mr. Alvarezo stopped. And stepped out
of the tree. Picked up his box and scissors. He clipped the rose and
put it in the box. He clipped at least twenty more along the rows
and he went inside. And then Awful got quiet.

"Daniel?" I rolled off my arm. I whispered "Now?"

He turned my way. "He's taking them to Mrs. Orofolo" he said.
The whole time I was counting roses and thinking about my arm he
was figuring that out. That was Daniel for you.

We went back over the brick wall. "Orofolo" Daniel said. Oh ROW
Fo Low was the way he said it.

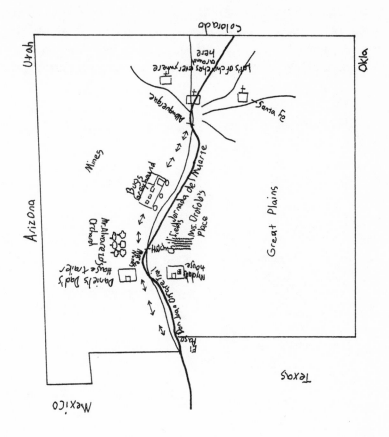

Bus's Bus Route

When I made the map I couldn't fit the 7-11 place which is in Hatch and which is where Bus parked to let people on and to give us stuff. He never talked except to Daniel who he talked secretly to. Daniel wouldn't tell me what it was. He said "Bus said not to tell."

New Mexico Mined

The President in those days which was the 1845s was James K. Polk and he wanted a war on Mexico so he declared one. Daniel said "It shall not be easy."

"No?"

The way it turned out it wasn't one bit. We cut across the highway and bellycrawled a corner of the chile field. You don't feel chile juice on you all at once because you just don't. But then. Oh man.

Mrs. Orofolo's place was one big room and an indoor john and a tree bigger than either one. She had a garden growing and it was neat and weedy and muddy and rotty too like a faceful of noserun. Daniel said muddy shoes would make his dad mad.

"It ain't going to make my dad grin" I said real quiet.

"You don't know."

I didn't. Sometimes you couldn't take the time to sit and think Daniel over. Sometimes he was 15000 years old. And I had a lot of questions I wished I asked. How come buffalos which there aren't many left except in zoos always got a look on their face like you just called on them in school? Did President Polk believe that stuff about the Seven Cities of Cibola? Did he just want a dead beaver hat like everybody else? What got into the Pueblos when they drew wings on snakes all over their jars? What was the whatever it was that Bus knew that Daniel told him that I didn't know? What about those Franciscan guys? How come they acted like they didn't know nothing about slavery and massacres and all? Why didn't somebody around 1706 invent the camera and take pictures? How come no Conquistador Women came over? Did they ever come over? Because you sure can't tell from the encyclopedia.

Mrs. Orofolo had a tall white picket fence around her willow tree. A little ropetie gate to it. And small purple flowers inside and not one weed. We crawled through the gate and into the circle of the must've been just painted pickets. The tree was so big around you couldn't hardly fit yourself between it and the fence, especially not with your whole frontside chilebaking.

She came in the kitchen with the rose basket. Mr. Alvarezo left it off for her and went I guess. She set the basket on the table and stepped back from it and took a big chestout whiff. It made her happy. You could tell. A kind of pinkness just spread over her. If you could've seen it I'll bet even her hump was the color of a baby's tongue.

Daniel gave me a look that said it was Some Adventure all right wasn't it?

Mexico didn't fire a shot which means it's got to be the easiest war ever. First the Mexicans gave up New Mexico Texas and California. Then there was some of New Mexico left so the U.S. got the southern part too by making a Gadsden Purchase. It was already 1853. I don't know what happened to President Polk because all of New Mexico is only 5 pages in the encyclopedia and Bert Trujillo had the Peking to Probability volume.

Mrs. Orofolo's name was not Therese. Daniel said that Therese's real name was Dorothy Therese Somebody. Mrs. O was sure happy anyway. She floated herself on to the only chair at her kitchen table. Scooted it back aways. Her hands crossed over her and each one unbuttoned the sleeves of her shirt. The hands went under the shirtsleeves and ran slow over her arms from elbows to wrists and back and over and under the way a praying mantis does to itself.

She unbuttoned her collar like you'd do something if you were showing somebody. She was showing the rose. That's what you'd have to figure. You know that little bowl where your chest stops and your neck starts going up? She touched that and then she kind of measured off every part of her neck and front and back with her palms and her fingers. She was pink as new gum.

I was ready to go. Daniel was solider than the tree—which meant he wasn't going with me no matter how good of a Miner Character I was. With just the tips of her fingers she felt of her nose and traced over her jaw. She turned her hand down and passed her thumbnail over her lips like she was going to kiss her own thumbnail. But she didn't.

She bent her head and closed her eyes which was the only time she wasn't looking at the roses. And you can only tell so much looking out a fence but I guess she had a great big breath of herself because it wasn't like she could breathe anything else with her head like that.

And she cried. Quiet and private—except for us right there not looking at her longer or not looking at each other or just undoing that perfect white gate and escaping like you always have to do in a real good adventure.

I made a lot of notecards about it. Pedro Castenada did too.

> It seems to me that this happened to all or most of those who went on the expedition which, in the year of our Savior, Jesus Christ, 1540, Francisco Vasquez led in search of the Seven Cities. Granted that they did not find the riches of which they had been told, they found a place in which to search for them and the beginning of a good country to settle in, so as to go on farther from there. Since they came back from the country which they conquered and abandoned, time has given them a chance to understand the direction and locality in which they were, and the borders of the good coun-try they had in their hands, and their hearts weep for having lost so favorable an opportunity.[5]

On the shoulder of the highway we slowed down. "Smarty" said Daniel. I thought he said Smarty but he never called me nothing but Chum or lad. The way he said it didn't make me mad or noth-ing I guess. Maybe almost mad. How was I supposed to know he was talking about his little sister Marty who you never hardly saw ever.

He stopped the way a state map will quit at the top. Colorado is up there but you don't see farther than Durango.

"Go on" I said or "Come on Daniel!" or something like it. I wasn't sure if I wanted to hear what he didn't say. A lot was hap-pening inside me. A lot was happening period.

In four years half of New Mexico was made The Territory of Arizona and cattle drivers drove cattle up and down the Goodnight-Loving Trail like Bus in his Greyhound.

27

Navahos were chased out of Arizona and captivated at Bosque Redondo. Kit Carson did it. They were starved plenty and tortured some too. 1864 to 1868. There was a mine boom. Mines were everywhere you stepped.

"Smarty" Daniel said in his omiscient voice. "I'm not going home." No lad stuff. No shall this or shall that.

I could've said "Daniel. You got to go home. What do you mean 'I'm not going home?' What's with this Smarty stuff? Daniel. Captain. Buddy. Hey."

The fact of it is that about as much time went by as you'd take to say such things and then I said "But I."

"You go ahead there." Did I say he had a burr haircut? "I got to look after Smarty." That's what he said. Whoever's got burr haircuts anymore? He really did have one. And when he meant something his whole head meant it.

That was 2 o'clock or so. I told him I could be around until supper if he was going to be around too.

"I'm not" he said. His voice was omiscient as all get out. A voice in a big deep jar.

I patted his shoulders is all I did. His face got Zuni! He punched my arm mean and kept punching and said "Don't—no—touch. No!"

So. I was going to punch him. I really was. Why not? But I said something my dad says. "Time wounds all heels."

He walked one way down the highway. I walked one way up it to home. That simple. His jacket was brown leather inside. It was red on the outside. I put some of it together. He was worried about his little sister.

It was real real simple.

After supper I couldn't hold back and I busted out crying and my dad said "About Daniel?"

"He ain't home even I bet."

"Tell me all you know" Dad said. He repairs small things. He likes to have every small part laying on the table in front of him.

When I finished he said "Stay here."

Nine or ten o'clock I was still hearing Dad's voice and Daniel's dad's voice call "Daniel! Daniel!" Over the cars on the highway even you could hear them. It should've been the saddest thing you'd ever hear. But his name was the most beautiful sound. Beautiful. I was thinking it when I fell asleep at the kitchen table.

On the next day which was Monday Daniel and I were back at school. "Found you" I said to him.

"Found me." Even Geronimo wasn't as sad when he said it.

All the cattle got mad after that. They shook their heads and said "It's got to stop. Up and back. Up and back." Their hoofs were sore. They had a revolt which was dusty and bloody.

They won. And that was the end of a twenty years cattle boom. And after that some more happened.

"We're moving." My dad said that a month later. "Orla."

It was out of the blue. Orla.

"In Texas where Grandpa lives."

"But" I said. "Daniel."

"You'll have to say so long to Daniel."

My Conclusion

And that's it complete. We didn't go to Orla because my dad met Bet in the Hayden's Hardware and she is my stepmother now. A Catholic. Nobody ever did make New Mexico a state which I know is hard to believe but a lot of things are come to think of it.

Daniel's dad wouldn't let me say good-bye. My dad had come with me to their trailer. "Joe" Daniel's dad said. "You've got it all wrong."

My dad held Daniel's hand. He said "Daniel. Everybody knows. Police. Teachers. Everybody. It'll stop now." He said "Is Marty in there?"

"Joe" said Daniel's dad. "For Christ's sake."

Then my dad said "Daniel. I can't take you with me. Listen. Daniel." But Daniel wouldn't listen. "The law says I can't take you." He came down to his knees like he did when he hugged me sometimes. But Daniel wouldn't hug him. My dad kneeled there and didn't get up. It was quiet. And even Daniel's dad was dust blowing over dust which is a sound that's no sound. And I don't think Marty was even around. My dad said to Daniel "Chum doesn't know." Then he stood up.

I didn't know what it was I didn't know. Daniel was crying too hard to talk or I bet he would have explained to me because I was his buddy and he wouldn't keep it from me if he knew how not to. It was something more terrible than a beating. That's what I learned later on.

Now my stepmother is going to type it up and she isn't sure about commas but she knows her quotation marks and such if you got to know which my dad says you do.

BIBLIOGRAPHY

Encyclopedia Brittanica Ed Ralph Twitchwell "New Mexico" 1962.

New Mexico Magazine October "Bosque Redondo"Dorotea Price
    1964.

National Geographic April "Mighty Lost Land" Clarence Boston
    1964.

The Relations of Alvar Nunez Cabeza de Vaca Ed Smith
    Buckingham Barn's Co. 1905. 1871.

Spaniard Americans Lucy Gonsalos University of New Mexico
    Albuquerque 1960.

Wild Land of Sun Andy Howe Wallace and Horn Albuquerque 1953.

Ice

"I want a big booth, on the window," I told the hostess, "away from the clock. I'm not in a hurry. I'm going to just park myself here." And think.

It seemed like everything I could ever think about was on the restaurant table before me. Spoon, fork, knife, wrapped in a napkin, bound in a paper ring. Disposable place mat. Cup on a saucer.

I had to eat, didn't I? Did eating at IHOP make me a monster? The cops would know soon enough. They'd find me. And what I did wouldn't be a crime if I said it wasn't. I was the LumberWorld company nurse—had been for twenty years. The procedure went wrong, and that happens. I was lancing a sty for a young man named Zack.

"I'm not ready to order yet. I need to look at the menu," I told the waitress. Dodie.

Or Dorie.

I was lancing a sty.

A two-page menu was on the table. A ketchup bottle. According to Heinz, America's favorite ketchup is Heinz. A card cleverly folded into a tent advertised The Earlybird Special.

Eggs Fresh. Ask Our Hens.

Zack's lower lid almost swelled the whole left eye closed. I taped his right eye shut. I said, "This will help," but didn't say who or what.

He said he was nervous.

I tapped my knuckle on his forehead. I asked, "You mean you're *afraid?*"

He didn't answer.

I said, "Of course." I said, "I'm not through with you, soldier." I pushed the surgical lance into the meat of his left eye, all the way in.

And I julienned his eyeball, more or less.

The cushions at my booth had the right firmness. The table, not a flimsy table at all, was covered with pieces of information. Equal Sweetener Tastes Like Sugar. No Steak Sauce Is Better. Quality Is Guaranteed. A bunch of propaganda.

The left eye. Four seconds is what it took. His upper eyelid closed over the lance, some kind of reflex probably, and I turned the blade inside his eye and sliced through the lid like the skin of a grape. He passed out.

I taped a gauze compress over the butchered eye.

I washed up.

I left.

And when he came to, what would he say? He had given me what people don't usually give a fat and unattractive woman: the benefit of the doubt. That was his mistake.

I wanted the real sugar, the regular coffee. I wanted the Farmer's Gold Seal half & half in those little white plastic cups. Another pat of butter. Another side of sausage. I wanted the maple, not the flavored syrup. I asked for juice with ice, and I wanted my ice. The waitress acted like I asked for the impossible.

When he first sat down, I taped the right eye shut. Because—he wouldn't look at me, and that happens to me, and I don't like it. I said, "What are *you* not looking at?" I moved Zack's head so he had to see me through the untaped eye. The bad one. It could be I have a pretty face. It could be I have a nice face. How would he know if he didn't look? He looked. Looked close.

I don't like that any more than I like being ignored. I said, "You're eighteen. Your name 's Zack. Single. Male." He had given me a one-page medical history. He was 5'6" or 5'7". Pleasant smile. No glasses or contacts.

He said, "You're pushing forty. Female. Your name's Johnson," which it was and which was always funny for the boys his draftable age who noticed my nurse's badge: My Name Is L. Johnson.

He asked, "Lynn? Lola?" He asked, "Ladybird? Loretta?"

"Are you going over there?" I asked. The Vietnam question. You couldn't not ask it. It's what you asked a fit boy that age.

I didn't like any of it. I thought, Dora, Dodie, Dina, if you ever come back to my table, I want you to know I wanted the meat cooked. I wanted the eggs runny. I didn't want my toast greased up.

My lipstick was fresh. I pressed my red lips together like I was spreading the color. I said, "I need you to take your shirt off. Here's a gown. And what do you do for LumberWorld, Zack?"

"Move boards from here to there," he said, "loading—unloading," and yanked his shirttails out and ducked his head in and pulled the shirt off.

I was taken by surprise. There was a flimsy cage where his upper body should have been. Bones. Bones and no flesh.

"And I'm a driver sometimes," he said. He saw me trying to look at his bare awfulness. His arms were skinny as broom handles.

I took the gown out of his fists, moved his puny arms away from his waxy-skinned narrow chest. "God," I said. "You're nearly starved."

Dora said, "You need anything?" I said, "Dodie. Dora. Is it Dora, dear?" I had my nurse's uniform on, which as far as I could tell, legitimized my scrutiny of people. I said, "I need to be less fat—don't even comment, okay?—and—here's a secret—I need to be less ugly. But I need to eat. You're fat, Dora, but *you* eat. You're ugly, but *you* eat. Right?"

He said, "I can't talk about it. I could maybe get in trouble with Selective Service."

I said, "Them. The national undertakers."

It was a nasty sty. A dark speck had made its own eye inside the swelling bubble of pus on his lower lid. It had closed his eye into a boxer's wink. If you touch one of these you can feel it pulse.

I pushed two fingertips against it. Zack whispered, "Hurts."

Dora marched off towards the Please Wait To Be Seated sign—an improbably big sign, a warning to all those who will not wait. Dora and the hostess huddled, and there was some pointing at me. Some frowning. There was some new and improved ugliness in Dora worse than the ugliness I saw before.

I said, "Tell me the rest—about Selective Service." It was none of my business. I stopped pushing on the sty.

He said, "You on the pill?" Yeah. Like that. It was his way of saying, My draft number is none of your business. Or it was a preemptive strike to keep me from asking anything at all about him, or it was a young man, afraid, saying, You show me yours, I'll show you mine.

I pushed hard again on the sty. "Little fucker," I said.

"Fair is fair," he said, his eye winking, his gaze focusing. He took the gown out of my hands, put it on.

What you do with one of these badly swollen stys is you make a lateral cut and you tweezer out the invasive stuff, and you press and press and then you pat to drain out everything. Most of the time you don't need to stitch. Young people heal fast. Isn't that what everybody always says?

He said, like he was a doctor, like I was his patient, "You're on the pill." I tied up the collar of the gown for him. The little white string. His neck was skinny as my daily newspaper.

He didn't know where to put his hands now that he wasn't holding the gown.

I had to make it up to Dora for being mean to her. I told the hostess, "Tell her I want to make it up to her."

I placed each of his hands on an armrest. I calmed them with my hands. And he spilled the beans. He had learned that if he lost forty pounds or more from his Standard Weight he would be ineligible no matter what number he drew. I said, "Your parents know?" They knew, he said, and said, "You don't know them. They'd do anything for me." Which meant they'd shut up and watch. And hope. And love their disappearing son. And hope. I know about that. I'm at that age now that I know what I remember about how my parents loved me, their strange one, their ugly child, and worried for me. They worried for me, and they loved me enough. You would think the beauty they helped me see in myself would save me from needing to recognize it through other people's eyes.

I said, "We don't freeze you for this procedure. It's a split-second thing." I unpackaged the surgical lance. I positioned the blade. I drew it across tissue that I pinched up with my fingertips. Expert. I tweezered out the cause of his problem. I pressed on the open eye of the wound. I thought about the way things are that a young person like that had to starve in order to live.

He looked at me the best he could with his wounded left eye. Penetrating but not cruel. He looked in, entered me like a large room, looked around to see what was on the walls.

Probably if you tape one eye shut the other immediately compensates by seeing what it never could. What's the science there? Complicated, I bet. He was diagnosing, I knew that. You have to be cold as snow on a thorn when you diagnose. I'm no doctor, but I know how the best, the most merciful ones measure it all. Mercilessly.

He whispered, "You don't want to be on the pill." It's a guess you could make about any woman my age with no wedding ring on. Any boy his age would speculate. That's the age they speculate about old virgins. It's what they do.

I reached behind him, pulled the little string knot tight. I whispered, "Why are we whispering?" That made him laugh.

I want more than one goddamn paper napkin. I'm greasy and I've spilled on myself, and if Dina or Dora or whoever won't wait on me I'm not paying. I told all that to the hostess.

I changed my mind about forgiving Zack. And that doesn't mean I didn't feel compassion for him. I wanted to help as much as I wanted to hurt.

"I'm going to the bathroom to clean up," I told the hostess. "You tell Dora I expect to see her at my table when I get out."

A miserable bathroom. Poor light. No vent. Bad tiling job. Smoke-stained mirrors. Some of that grout, some of that smoke, air, light, some of it must have been twenty years old. A toilet the size of a toy. Whose ass fits toilets like that?

I loosened the knot around his blushing throat. "And what's the rest? What's your weight?" I asked. "How much've you lost?"

He made his best effort not to look. Lasted one second. He looked up my arms. He looked at my face. Not a nice face. Not pretty. Not at all. Tried to look at my breasts through my blouse. Eighteen. God. Boys're just one giant infected eye at that age.

The boltless door to the only bathroom stall was gummy—on both sides. The sink, with a bull's-eye of green scum inside a target of lighter green, gurgled. My face in the mirror was so far away from the face in my mind. The towel dispenser, which said, Clean Every Time, was empty.

He sunk back in the chair. I was glad I had taped the right eye shut. He wouldn't look at me anyway. He looked over my shoulder, like he saw something behind me sweep into his view then sweep out.

I said, "Oh, Zack. The weight—your weight. You haven't lost enough, have you?"

He said, "I can't lose it fast enough." Without looking at me, he looked like he saw in me the whole world's disinterested way of numbering boys like him. "I'm nervous," he said.

I tapped my knuckle on his forehead. I asked, "You mean you're *afraid?*"

He didn't answer.

I said, "Of course."

That's when I unpackaged the second surgical lance. That's when I said, "I'm not through with you, soldier."

Smoke

The doctor said that my eye drifted. Lazy, he said. A lazy eye that must be taught—he said this to my eye itself. "You will make this eye act correctly if you are a determined young man. And are you?"

Floater, my friends, including my good friends, called me, and that was no crueler or kinder of them than of any eleven-year-olds in my town. The left eye was like a small raft on uncalm water, and while it worked for seeing, I had never been able to move it where I wished, not since birth, no matter how hard I rowed across the faces of my parents and teachers, or across the pages in the books I hungrily read.

I could see properly but I could never look like I was properly seeing.

The doctor showed me a light blue rubber ball, the size of a baseball, with a little U-nail pushed into it. He showed me a long elastic band that could be threaded through the U-nail. On the latitudes of the southern hemisphere of the ball he had handwritten the letters A, B, C, D, E, F, G, H, I, J, K, L in green, with the letter A at the south pole. On the northern latitudes he had written the numbers 0 through 11 in black, with 0 at the north pole. Two simple stories.

He was an eye doctor, different from the doctor who had treated me for smoke inhalation in the hospital two years earlier. As I lay on the examining table, he attached the top of the ball to the elastic band, then the band to the fluorescent light fixture attached to the ceiling.

He swung the ball at an angle across me, so that it passed by my face and shoulder and flew off beyond the range of my peripheral vision. He said, "Read the bottom when it passes." I could read the A but none of the other letters on the spinning ball.

He stopped it in its flight, held it in his fist, and looked at it without looking at me. He swung the ball in a circle around my whole body. As it wound a closer and tighter circle around the center of me and close around my head, very close, and around my face, my nose, he said, "Read."

He impatiently explained my schedule: half an hour of the southern hemisphere, and the strenuous effort to see the ball and the letters when they were close and when they were in the distant periphery; half an hour of the northern hemisphere, and absolute concentration on the numbers as they circled me.

He was a tough one. It was the early sixties, and the dentists and doctors in our town must have all received the same military medical training because they gave orders and they expected results. He did not bring my mother into the room to explain. He did not want to have to see her, answer her questions. He asked me, "You can tell your parents about all of this?"

I had the ball in one hand. I had the elastic band in the other. I was on my back, my eye drifting. The words, "if you are a determined young man," echoed in me. I did not look as if I understood anything. I had never seen him before, would probably never see him again, and why should I care if he did not meet my parents who were both highway-construction workers and more "determined" than anyone he had ever met. He did not ask about the smoke in my lungs, though he had my medical file on his small metal desk. I had been told by the hospital doctor that my lungs would recover from the damage. When they were healthy once more I would have no problem with the smoke that would, according to him, always remain in me.

I did not tell my mother or father the part about the eye doctor calling the eye lazy. I never told them about being called Floater at school. I told them everything about the light blue rubber ball, my routine, my schedule.

My father insisted on lying down next to me on my bed so I

could show him how it all worked. He asked how it would ever be possible to see the numbers at the very top of the ball.

I showed him that when the ball was at a particular distance and angle in its orbit you could see to the very top: 0. You had to anticipate that brief moment. It was easy to see the A at the bottom, and possible, depending on the spin, to see the B, C, and some of the other letters. The letters and the numbers were like landmasses on a globe.

"An hour of this every day, Zack, and you could start seeing the future," he joked.

"Get up," my mother said to him because it was not quite right for him to be on my bed. I had never seen him like that. I had never seen him or my mother on any bed. I'm not sure even now—now that I'm the age they were then—that they ever rested.

My father ignored her. He looked up at the ceiling of my room where he would put the hook. From that position on the bed, he looked at the three walls and even seemed to look at the one behind him, all without moving his head or his sun-blackened neck. "*This,*" he said, "is a solid place." He said it firmly. He was defensive of my mother who blamed herself for the kitchen fire that had trapped me in my room for a short while and had burned more than half of our house down, and he was defensive about the reconstruction and the plumbing that he and a friend of the family had done. It had taken them two years. My mother's youngest brother, D.A., did all the electrical. Earlier that same year there had been a terrible fight between D.A. and Mother, and this was a way for both of them to make it right. It took almost a year to redo the wiring Uncle D.A. had done.

Later that afternoon, when I hung the ball back up on the ceiling hook, my father stood next to my bed and watched. "Plumb," he said. It was not a comment on the ball, the ceiling, any of that. It was about the world, our family's situation, our place in the big picture. Things were "Plumb" or "Out of plumb" as far as he was concerned. Because of his nature and his peculiar form of optimism, it took a lot to convince him that anything was ever really out of plumb.

Before dinner, he and my mother sat on the same large, worn wingback chair in the living room. She sat next to him but almost in his lap; her left shoulder blade rested against his chest; her cheek was near and sometimes against his. Most evenings, they read library books to each other on that chair, which was old and smoke-damaged. Our dog, Cookie, regularly attended their little service, probably because he found their voices soothing, or because he particularly valued the *Reader's Digest* condensed form. It was important to them that I know they read to each other from the Bible even if they never read it in that chair. They were churchgoers, but not the usual troubled, undetermined believers. They believed.

In my room I had swung the blue ball too fast. I swung it more slowly. I heard them reading. Usually I sat on the floor near them, and listened to their expressive voices, night fires sending up tiny sizzling sparks. On top of the vinyl ottoman, Cookie gnawed and scratched himself, making enlightened grrrring noises. They read one chapter only, less than ten pages. There was no discussion, but there was no lost sense of connection in the silence.

I could smell the dumplings expanding in the yellow unclarified soup of celery and onions and paprika-rubbed chicken barely still on the bone at the bottom of the cooking pot in the kitchen. Lemons were halved and crushed and the pulp scraped out. The long wooden spoon knocked the sides of the green plastic lemonade pitcher Uncle D.A.'s wife Cathy had given us.

I knew that my mother, who usually just called me to supper, would come to my room to talk with me.

I could not see her when she stood at my doorway in order to watch me finish my routine. From an underside view, I was straining to see the numbers 9, 10, 11 at the middle of the equator as the ball circled beyond my vision and into my vision and beyond again. I knew that with practice I could learn to track the ball's every movement over me. I would eventually flinch less and keep my head still and learn how to breathe a certain way that made inhaling and exhaling part of seeing. I would see farther into the periphery.

She said, "Is it hard to do?" She meant that it was *not* hard for a young man as determined as me.

"I'm trying to concentrate," I said. "Sorry," she said. "Well. Concentrate."

The ball circling my face counterclockwise caused thrilling dizziness and blurring. Nothing was visible to me on either hemisphere. I began to think I saw the circling ball bisect, the north swing out of sync across the south. When everything slowed, then reconciled, I recited what I saw: A, B, C, D, E, F, G, H, I, J, K, L, 11, 10, 9, 8. That was as far as I could get.

I did not see my mother's melted hand, the keloid gloss on her fused thumb and first finger, the other fingers missing. I did not see the drying spoon held waist-high in her other hand. I had seen all of it before, and I can remember it now, that closed bird claw of her left hand, the bits of damp pulp on the spoon, her pencil grip on the warped rough wooden stem, a kind of writing motion she made with both hands, and a smile that always seemed related to that motion.

I swung the ball out clockwise, out beyond my toes and head. It lightly brushed the walls of the room. "Oh," she said, with so much pleasure. "Oh, *son*," with such joy.

My sense of awe increased. Though only by a small fraction, it increased.

And I felt amazed at her. She showed no sadness, not a trace, though she had all but lost that hand, and she and my father, uninsured, had lost through the fire or the smoke or the water damage everything, including their used Bug in the garage.

I had not thought much about the fire except as a thing that had thrown us only a little out of plumb, and for only a short while. The fire happened. Two years later they rebuilt. My mother joined my father on the construction crew. With no money to spare, they sent me to the eye doctor.

I can remember now, with great particularity, what I was almost oblivious to then, on that first day of exercising my eye. My mother was making food in a pot she had been given by a friend of the family. My father was sitting on one of the two pieces of furniture in the living room. Cookie had just jumped off the other piece that was unmatched because each piece had come from a different friend of the family. There were wall plates on the light switches in my room, but in no other rooms yet. There was not a desk, not a chest of drawers and a reading lamp in their room as there was in mine. There was a mattress on their floor, not a new bed and frame. I had clothes in my closet, dress shoes and tennis shoes.

I practiced every day for two years until I was thirteen, which was the only other time I saw the eye doctor. He held a mirror before me and asked me to see for myself if I was "correct." He did not quite believe.

I knew it was hopeless to explain to him that from my first day with the ball, I no longer cared if I would look like I was properly seeing. I wanted to see beyond.

I would not be able to explain to him how the ball made a sound swinging over me, a breathing counterpoint to my breathing. The world, our situation, all of that, inside and outside of me, seemed projected onto the ball. I would see farther and farther into the periphery. I was determined. I saw along the blue curve to the larger numbers, 11, 10, 9, 8, 7, 6, and, eventually, to the smaller ones, and, when that world was at a certain distance and angle, I saw the black zero at the very pole.

Been So Good to Me

We were belted in. At the proper limit. Passing no one. One long hour away from El Paso International Airport. I drove because Harry said he needed to sleep, but I knew he was wide awake and pretending as we both had been for years.

I made conversation with myself and the dairy cows at the brinks of their pens, their heads swimming from the chemical feed and the afternoon sun and the vertigo of having no freedom from each other. I asked them if they ever stopped—making milk, making milk. They shook their beautiful but cowish heads, gave each other that holy wooden look. Of all the things I thought the cows might want—I thought of that—I thought, What do you need? I believed they might want music most. I popped in my favorite tape.

Lord! Lord! Lord! Lord! Lord, you been good to me.
You sure been good to me.

The Five Blind Boys. Oh, cows, I said. There is this one good thing. One. *Lord. Lord. Lord. Lord.*

Want to sing? I asked the cows. We can sing with The Boys—that might be something new.

Harry should have been laughing, my unmoving friend. Or grinning. He should've. He could've given me that much at the end of our friendship.

The windows closed, the air on, windshield clean, the commotion narrowing, the path inside widening, I wished again I was a teacher giving a lesson, a man making a wish at the well in the heart of a friend. I wished, too, I had sunglasses like The Five Blind Boys do, and I wished them well wherever they were now, at least seventy or eighty years old, rocking some First African Methodist Episcopal, or making tears flow at a riverside funeral, or knocking their own canes at the gates of heaven, the blue sheen of their suits blinding the faithful welcomed, at last, over heaven's borders.

Sure been good to me.
Been so good to me.

How, I wanted to know, were men with the same thirst brought together, gathering other thirsting men around them? How did five blind boys find each other? At what school? At what old pine shack or glory tent pitched on what small town's outskirts? Which one cast his voice out first to bring in what he couldn't see, and then felt that bell strike on his face, another boy singing.

What age were they then? Seven or eight? Two of them searching out the vacant field, climbing the gum tree there in the hot sun and singing all the way up.

It makes no difference a-what you say—
I'm a-goin on my knees and pray—

Never calling it practice, but singing away and over and over, practicing more at the top, dawn fire and dusk on their faces and in the star-shaped leaves on the fingers of the branches.

And I'm gonna wait—a-wait right here—
Until he comes.

And the two decided there should be a third for some belly to go with the heart and head.

He's my rock, my sword, my shield—
He's my wheel in the middle of the world—

Boys, their worried parents asked. Think. Where'll it lead?

It led them into the tree. Hands clasped into stirrups, shoulders made into steps to launch each other up. They smelled the tree pitch and each other's intermixed sweat, and laughed at the stink. The new boy asked, When do we sing?

Whenever we want, they said. From the first branch of the First Church of the Gum Tree they started "Somewhere Listening for My Name." Where slight and strong branches overlapped, the new boy asked, D'you either one preach?

Aww, yes, Lord, yes, they said, but neither one did when he called them out on it. They sang, *And I'm a-gonna wait—a-wait right here—Until He comes.* The new boy had bottom when he joined in, and joined at just the right time. They rested on an uncurved unstable black limb.

Alligator skin, said one.

The other said, Must've been found by lightning.

The first said, Ain't safe.

The other said, What is?

The new one whispered, I could go ahead?

They thought he meant to climb. But he tuned his voice— Hooom!—and did a dead-on talking gospel.

This train is known as The White Flyer to Heaven. God is the engineer—and the Holy Ghost is the headlight. No liars can ride on this train! No deceivers can ride on this train.

That adds on, one said. Still. Heck, I don't know. The other said, I don't either. But both of them did.

Three blind boys. Crowned in branching darkness and reigning over it with each other.

The dairies along the highway south to El Paso never end. The cowshit, in mounds fifteen feet high, is covered with black tarp and the tarp with tires and the tires with sand, and it all looks like a bombed burial ground. Currents of sand blow over the cows, who stumble and hold still and bow and kneel like evaporating spirits. And sing.

I say they sing. They can if I say. I have kicked my shovel into my heart, and I am digging.

My cruise control is on. My wrists and arms rest. I say to my un-sleeping, undreaming friend, You're pretending. You should wake up, smell the cows. You can't beat cows. You can't. What good would it do?

I imagine that adding another boy was never planned. They went up the gum. They came down. Sang. Climbed. Sermonized. Nine or ten years old by then. Needed more songs. Found people with record players who wanted to share, but wanted to hear, too, and said, Come down here, you boys.

Need the tree, the boys said. And ascended, and sang down to their wiseass friends who asked, You take requests? and to their folks who shouted up, We never knew! and who brought them food, and said they would leave, but couldn't help themselves and stayed.

And people filled that empty field.

Miracle, they said. You heard them, too? You heard?

Two years like that. And crowds gathering under the gum tree Sunday mornings and sometimes late, late in the weekday eve-nings. You come, the old ones commanded their grandchildren, come hear what God done to those blind boys. Up there. *Oh, Father, Father.* And, because of the music's deepness and the boys' blind-ness, no one asked should those boys be so far up in the darkness.

One singing night one boy stepped on the alligator branch, and he stayed safe but sent it crashing down. People fell upon the ashes of that broken black angel, and when they learned the boys up in the tree were all right, they wept, moaned, screamed, danced. They danced. Everyone sang. They sang out and danced around from that day on every time the boys sang down.

The preacher one said every night, I could go ahead? And— Hoom!—he did—said, *Sometime on this peaceful journey, friends, my burden get a little heavy,* and they sang, *Yooooouuuu!* and he said, *I have to steal away and talk to my God and your God—tell Him all about my troubles*—and they sang, *know myyyyyyyy!*—Say it! Say it out!—*soooouuuul!*

If you say it out what *can* happen happens.

Two swaying boys on the ground below them howled with them to beat hell back. And stretched their small arms and hands, and lifted their blind eyes, and no one asked when they had come or where from as they were raised up by silent women and men into the arms of the three above.

Five blind boys.

Benches went up for the elders, and the elders who just knew and needed no reason, started bringing small rooted canes of roses.

Yoooouuuu know myyyyyyy soooouuuul—looks back in wonder.

Wake up! I said, nearly shouted to Harry, pretending and awake, long-loved and lost—of us two cruel men, the cruelest. What do you need? I want you to have that.

So many climbing roses reached up even into the gum tree's highest branches, no one could find the boys inside that color unless they listened for the singing streaming through it. And how could those boys find each other then except by singing, except by hearing?

(All lyrics traditional: versions by The Fairfield Four, Reverend A.W. Nix, The Golden Eagle Gospel Singers, and The Five Blind Boys of Mississippi.)

Make it sound like a train

Make it sound like a train, the woman said. I want to make it sound like a train. She banged again on the open D.

Preacher was not a young man, she was not a young, unknowing woman. She knew. He knew. He was supposed to teach.

In order to stall, he asked, An old train on new sunlit track? A train in a tunnel at night? A train drawing a golden line across the dark?

Not what I had in mind, she said.

An empty train in a sentenced man's dream on an empty prison bed? Train in a bottle? On a trestle of planks in a basement or barn? The last, best, first run on a virgin line, the engine groaning all morning long under the hard kisses of the sleet and the wind's assault?

She asked him, What?

He said, I don't know what you need, whether or not you want a train with a load of church brick or Sheetrock or baby crib or the unpaid debt, the unjust doubt, the guiltlust of men who teach women who ask to be taught how to sound like a train that a man might have caught on a track he took seemed like a hundred years ago.

Like a train, she whispered, *like a train*, wanting to tell Preacher, wanting him to tell in one lesson the key, the first, the fourth and fifth chords, the turnaround, the tempo, the words for how to find the song outside the sound inside and go, just go.

You don't know? she asked.

He didn't.

Hoom! he said.

He put her hands, fingers, the strap on her lovely shoulders where they belonged, said, Hitch your thumb here, curl your hand, lower your elbow. Rest your arm on the belly, your heart on the bend. Lower your head, skid onto your mark there with the bottle-glass slide.

Here?

Here. And only tap, ride up to it, down from it, then dampen the sound with your palm or your thumb. And not so strong, so soon, not so soon, so strong.

He said, Don't start with that, but she'd begun.

I'm going down south, child,
this weather it gets too cold.
I'm going down south, child,
this weather it gets too cold.
Done laid round Chicago—
I ain't got a change of clothes.

He asked her not to sing, not yet, but she wouldn't stop, so he said, Listen, here's what you do, here's what you do. You make one word sound like a woman, one like a man, one like a ghost of the two. Said, Kinda like this.

I had *thirty* days in JAIL, *child,*
my *back* turned TO the *wall.*
I had *thirty* days in JAIL, *child,*
my *back* turned TO the *wall.*

He said, Try this country blues thing here, tapped his foot in a one-two-and one-two-and beat. She played rough the way women will do who wish they were only playing. When he asked her to trap and tampen the sound with a lighter touch, she said, Like a train. He said, Like a train, saying, *One*-two-and *one*-two-and *choo*-chugga *choo*-chugga *down*-up *down*-up, steaming beyond them both while he watched her slam the downbeat, sing,

I'm leavin' this mornin—
got to shake your hand.

I'm leavin' this mornin—
got to shake your hand.
I'm goin to my woman—
you go back to your man.

He said, You sound like a ripped fan belt. Sound like a trip up a river on a leaky raft. Like a warden's laugh. Like death by flatpick. Play that again but not like that. And he showed her, singing,

*Leav*in this *morn*in—
Got to *shake* your hand.
*Leav*in this mornin—
Got to *shake* your hand.

She played—Preacher said, You sound about like my tapping foot, like disco, about like the clickclump of a broken heel tip or a liar's heartbeat, about like your hand got caught in a chain saw.

She said, So. Show me. She hit, smoothed out, lifted the bassackwards half of G, the root note ringing, left it.

So, she said. So. Show me.

He could.

He couldn't.

Preacher's hand, his head, his skin hurt from the sound he made, but he had said he would teach her—that's what he had said.

You have to saw through wood *in*side you, he said, *in*side you up to the nut.

So—so, she said, offer me shit, stall me with all that, keep asking me what when I'm asking you when, you fuck. And she knocked his big hand off its place of rest, gave his little hand a twist, shook his wrist loose with her wrist.

He wanted to say in four-four: Stop. Stop. Stop. Stop.

He showed her how she could brush her ring-finger bottle down the third rail to the twelfth, up to the seventh, hold out, tampen down, scream back to the switch, glide up to the nut into the station. He knew her guts stirred as soon as she felt what rushed from the strings into the hungry mouth, out.

Her head lowered, her glass finger came up under, under, onto the soft top of the C, made one tremolo thriller choo-*chug*ga choo-*chug*ga. The wrong strings buzzed light on the wrong but right fret, struck in the tempo of a featherweight tornado touching down to hit the wrong *beat* the wrong *beat* the wrong *beat* on a different truer track than the track Preacher ran on *next* to her *next* to her in a batswing thump*spin*, a hammer-*on*, a hammer-*on*, a one-note bend, a ghost-limb lowlonesome pull-off G-chord moan.

She didn't need to ask what that was about.

He didn't need to ask what that was about.

That was a train, she said.

He said, Whooooooshit. It sure was, wasn't it?

(Lyrics, Muddy Waters)

Permission

When Agnes and Jo and I asked if he was any good, the old man flattened his dark black hands against the oak bartop and looked down at them. A bar like U Dam Right is a place where you notice people's hands—what's on them, in them, whether they're empty. He pushed his hands farther out of his golden rayon shirtsleeves and said to bring him two shot glasses. "Never mind," he said and produced them out of the blue, snapping them down on the wood.

Flawless manicure. Some kind of clear polish on his pink nails. The backs of his hands and his fingers were bare. You could see dark hair on his wrists, but his hands—he had to have shaved his hands clean to make them look like that.

Agnes and Jo poured the salt into the shot glasses the way he asked, to the brim. He said starting at age fourteen he had been a bar magician, following the Rabbits Foot Minstrels and The Florida Cotton Blossom Show and Fletcher Henderson's Orchestra with Ma Rainey in the 1920s and Bessie Smith in the '30s. Permission the Magician.

"Only thing was—I'm warning you," he said, "it was all bawdy magic."

We shrugged.

He said, "I'm warning you."

What did we expect? We expected nothing. Nothing. I don't know. Not for him to lick the tips of his index fingers, dip them in the salt, say, "With your permission," and rub them over our lips. Not for him to have those polished silver front teeth when he smiled.

"Is that salt?" he asked.

Agnes and Jo said, "*What?* What?" said, "Salt."

I said, "Mmm-hmm. Salt."

I heard somebody else in the room say, *Salt.* There are always new echoes inside old echoes in a bar like this. Every bar has a ghost or two.

Permission said, "Ma Rainey sang—ever heard floodwater ripping out old foundations? She sang somethin' like that. Bessie was only about seventeen years old—she didn't know nothin' you compare her to Ma Rainey about then." He upended the shot glasses, righted them, and they were still full. "Pardon me," he said, and he offered one to Agnes and one to Jo and me. "Now we put our tongues in," he said.

"Not me," said Jo.

"Warned you," he said. Behind his frown the glint disappeared.

Jo held the shot glass between her and me. She caved. She was like that, giving nothing and everything and nothing again, always swiftly and in that order. I knew. I knew.

Our tongues went in, touched. And her forehead and my cheek.

Agnes and Permission put their tongues in. Agnes said, "It's sugar!" She was blushing. That was no big magic since Agnes, unmarried, in her late thirties back then, was always giving everything and getting nothing back, and feeling self-conscious about it. Every regular in the place knew.

Permission took the two glasses, held them over his head, his sleeves dropping like gilt curtains toward his elbows. His lips glistened with salt and sugar crystals he had not wiped away. He offered the glasses. "With your permission," he said. We had to put our tongues in again. In one glass there was tequila. In one was sugar.

He didn't ask what we tasted. He scrutinized us, like we were weak drinks he'd just finished.

"Should've heard," he said. "Bessie had twice Ma's loudness but none of her real power. She could make weather but she couldn't change the season. When Ma showed the band how to help Bessie shift her sound into the loudest part of her range, oh, now, my Lord!"

He lifted the glasses away, didn't give me time to stop him from pouring the sugar and tequila in one downpour onto the bar. It didn't matter. It was all salt when it hit.

Agnes said, "It—it's—" She pointed. She pointed so we could see Permission's missing middle finger on his right hand.

Jo had taken off her horrible glasses, these thick porthole things she wore. Horrible. She put them back on. She said, "Where did it go?"

"Wadn't ever there." Permission had a cloth the same material and color of his shirt. Magicians all have a cloth they work magic under. He pulled it from his pant pocket, used it then to polish the nub where the middle knuckle should have been. "Born 'thout."

I asked, "Is that why—"

"I had something to prove," he said. "Yeah. It's always that simple, ain't it, Bud?"

In a bar the blinds are drawn, the books aren't open, there is no loss margin. I had to ask how a person could have made a living as a bar magician. The next Friday that he came, he explained.

The bargoers didn't pay him for the act, but they could tip him. The bar provided him with food and booze. The singers and musicians gave him a nickel on every dollar at the door, put him up with them wherever they stayed.

He showed us a trick he could do with a five-dollar bill if Agnes would "let a old man get personal."

Agnes asked, "Personal?"

He said, "Mighty."

She smoothed her hands over her hips like she was measuring her own willingness. "Why not?" she said, and looked at Jo and me for the answer we couldn't give.

Permission folded up the bill with that magician flourish, like folding a bill was already magic. He said, "Picture this. Louis Armstrong is one of Ma's cornet players, and he doesn't know jack yet but he's workin' harder than all the rest. He's watchin' Joe Smith and Coleman Hawkins who knows some shit but who's watchin' Bessie Smith who's watchin' Ma Rainey who's singing, 'Countin' the Blues.' Ma's big legs is apart and her big body grindin' up against somethin' good she knows like nobody else. You ever heard Trixie Smith sing, *'My man rocks me with one steady roll'*? That's Trixie—seen Ma Rainey a hundred times—Trixie imaginin' she was Ma."

He had folded the bill until it was the size of a postage stamp. He said to Agnes, "Get yourself ready, girl. Next Friday."

A week later, he held up the folded bill. "Now, Agnes, I got to put Abraham Lincoln between your knees for this," he said. Agnes and Jo wore long red velvet waitress skirts with slits up to their waists and silk black frill along the edges of the slits. Agnes said, "I got hose on," which meant something only to her. She put both hands on my head, and she grinned at me.

About a week before, Agnes and I had sat a drunk, a small, flat-headed guy, against his car, or somebody's car anyway, and we put our hands on his head to get him upright and hold him that way, but he fell over, and Agnes and I fell into each other and together we took off her glasses and we kissed, and she said, "Is that what it feels like?" and I think now she probably meant love. But how could I tell then? And I didn't ask.

Permission had her sit with her legs together on a stool next to him. It was about 1:45 in the A.M. and quiet. A bar is like a long unlighted bridge with night over it and dark water under it cooling the blackness. I said, "You want more light?"—as if a magician ever wants that.

"With your permission," he said, his hands moving from the inside of her feet upwards, then his hands on the backs of her legs, smoothing her. "One night," he said, "Ma Rainey asks Louis to put a mute on. Louis ain't no good with it at all. And on the break he says, 'Aw, honey, why tie my hands behind my back?' She laughs, says, 'I like a man on a spit.' He says, all sparked, 'Why?' She says, 'You playing pretty but you ain't modulatin'.'"

Firmly, Agnes said to him, "Far enough."

Permission said, "Hold the bill tight there between your knees. You got it?"

Agnes pulled the skirt together—with Permission's hands still under it. "Got it."

Under the skirt he moved his hands down her legs, down the front and back of her legs and over her ankles and out from under the skirt. "Louis got the technique later, but he took ahold of the idea right there: Don't play so much. You put the mute in your hand it's remindin' you to leave things off. You play through it or around it, draw it off, clap it on, you're playin' the sound same time as you're playin' the silence."

Permission rubbed his black, hairless hands together. "Mr. Lincoln," he said to Agnes's closed skirt, "you in there?" He asked Agnes, "He in there?"

"Yep."

"You both havin a good time?" He said, "No travelin' upstate now, Abe!" He said, "So that's how come you hear Louis Armstrong saying to his band, 'That's some modulatin!' on his own records— that's how come. Because of what he learned from Ma Rainey."

He sang a little: *"I looked at the clock and the clock struck one. I said, 'Now, Baby, ain't we havin' fun?' My man rocks me with one steady roll."* He told Agnes she could ask Abe to leave if she wanted. "Open up," he said.

"Huh?"

"Open, open, ses-a-me." He nodded slowly at her lap instead of drawing a wand over her, but it had the same effect.

She opened the skirt and her handsome long legs. She touched her knees, then the inside of her thighs. She closed the skirt, crossed her legs. There was no bill there, of course.

Permission sang, *"I looked at the clock and the clock struck six. I said, 'Now, Baby, I like your tricks!'"* Permission said, "Nice shoes," and nodded slowly at her red spike heels, which was all it took for her to discover the unfolded bill against her right instep. Inside her hose.

He wanted a job at U Dam Right. "You want a job here?" I asked. "Here?"

We couldn't give him a job. After hours, when the whole crew was gone, I walked him to his car. Not good. A bumperless '81 Maverick with the hood missing, engine exposed, tires bald. I tried to explain how nothing was the same as in his day. Women and men didn't come to a bar like this for the music or even the dancing. They'd talk right through Alberta Hunter and Billie Holiday, and they'd ignore Ma Rainey even if she and her band nearly killed them with their sound. Women and men didn't need a magician to help them lower their inhibitions either. "It's all different everywhere between women and men," I explained as if what I believed was true for everybody.

He said, "What about you and Agnes?"

"We work together."

"Jo and you?" he asked.

I didn't answer.

"Jo and Agnes?"

"Give me a break," I said.

I didn't understand at all about women and men, that's what he was letting me know. I almost had a new college degree that I had never wanted in Business Administration and this bar-manager job to stay alive, and I had no clue. I was always offering people everything of the great nothing I knew. That's why a bar seemed like the way. The way for me to go.

Permission said, "How long we known each other, Bud?"

Before I could say six or seven hours over the past three weeks, he said, "Long time." Before I could say six or seven hours, tell him I was only twenty-three years old, before I could ask, "Are you sure you're all right?" he said, "You oughta know what I'm worth. I could be the boss card in your hand."

"I'm sorry," I said, "I can't hire you." The apology didn't take. "Permission—I'm sorry."

"Why do the men and women come here?" he asked, pretty obviously peeved at me.

I said, "They don't know. You look at them and you can see it. They don't know." But that wasn't exactly true. Like Jo and Agnes and me, people came here in order to hook up without having to know. We wanted to stay alive but not live. We wanted excuses not to be in love. A bar is like a wooden ladder you carry to a fire.

A bar is like an oar you keep in your car. He returned every Friday about midnight. He never showed us the same trick twice.

He could talk all night. He told us almost the whole story you never hear about the blues of the twenties modulating into the swing and dust-bowl folk and the bluesy gospel of the thirties and forties while it was modulating into the jazz of the fifties and the rockabilly and into rock'n'roll. He was obsessed with Ma Rainey and Bessie Smith, the Eve and Eve of the garden of American music. He said they were plenty more important than Charlie Patton and Son House and Robert Johnson and all the guys you hear about, even W. C. Handy.

After a year of this, I had to ask, "What are you after?"

"Same as you," he said.

"A buck? Free drinks?"

He said, "Well, them too." And he said, "I can show you if you look close. You won't look close, Bud. Go get the girls."

It was 2:30 A.M., and Jo and Agnes had changed into their street clothes. Jo said, "I have to get to sleep."

"Sleep through my magic if you want," he said.

"No."

"I'll put a spell on you," he said. "It can be done."

"Okay," she said, that simply, and stayed.

Agnes, who had already sat on the stool to his right, who had seen what he could do without a wand and without a middle finger on his right hand, pleaded, "Do the magic to me."

Jo selfishly said, "Me."

I said, "Me. Please."

A bar is a cannibal's kitchen. A bar is a suicide's garden. A magician's one true church. He pulled out the gold cloth. He snapped three shot glasses down on the bartop. In an instant they were already hidden under the cloth, mouths open but covered. He said, "With your permission," took Jo's lit cigarette, drew hard on it, gave it back. "Nice shoes," he said to Agnes. She looked at her shoes and so did we, and there was no magic there.

He laughed, exhaled smoke, said, "You so easy."

He said, "After Bessie's funeral—she got killed in a car accident—Clarksdale, Mississippi in '37—Ma Rainey organized a street parade on Hook Road outside Philadelphia, and marched out front and tried to sing happy like they do in New Orleans so people still alive get back to livin'. She moaned the tune and you only heard her singin', '*Nobody loves you when you're down and out*' if you heard it inside you. Louis didn't once lift the mute off his cornet. A sound like bees cryin'. Bessie's band had a guy in it that she'd taught to do her voicing when she left off singin'. He played his cornet into and out of the sadness like a new scissors cuttin' it all up into confetti. That was Ed Allen. Walkin' next to him, with his useless hands in his pockets, was Clarence Williams, who played piano sometime for Bessie."

Smoke rose out of the three covered mouths of the shot glasses on the bar. Permission told us, "Put your left hand on one—palms up—before the smoke disappears."

He sang, "*If I ever get my hands on a dollar again, I'm gonna hold on to it til them eagles grin.*" The little puff of smoke on the back of my hand was warmer than I thought it would be. My hand was in the middle; Agnes's was on the left; Jo's on the right.

He said, "Give your hand a kiss. Long kiss."

Jo said, "Are we having fun?" but lowered her face and roughly kissed her hand. Her hair, coarse as rug fiber, swung from her neck and hid her then. If you did not know her she would not look pretty to you. The thick glasses. That hair. If you did know her, she was too lovely to describe.

"Long kiss," Permission said.

I could see how lightly Agnes kissed herself. I could smell her powdery, chemical perfume. I could feel the decreasing heat in my hand against my lips, which were moist but drying.

Our faces were so close they were almost joined, but when we all at once started to lift our heads, he said, "Don't. Not yet."

He sang, "*Yeah, I'm gonna hold on to it til them eagles grin.*" By now, we had figured out that his storytelling was just a distraction, and his singing was the same. He told the old story about Bessie dying by bleeding to death because the white doctors in Clarksdale wouldn't treat her injured arm. He told us her headstone was stolen and, years later, a new one paid for by "a kindly lady named Janis

Joplin." He said, "I want you to kiss long, close your eyes. Close your eyes, kiss long, count ten."

He must have repeated himself or I must have repeated his words because I heard the words again in the room: *Close your eyes, kiss long, count ten.*

I closed my eyes and felt or heard Agnes close hers, which I know is impossible but I did. My hand was cooler. Janis Joplin came to mind. I wondered who paid for Janis's headstone. My lips were real dry and cool inside my palm, which was getting down-right cold. I swallowed hard, heard Jo swallow the same thirsting way. The coldness in my hand, painful, really painful, reached into my whole face. Jo's hair against my forehead and cheek was cold. Agnes's cheek against my own cheek and jaw was cold. She said, "Two. Three."

Permission yanked the cloth from under our hands, which were flat against the bartop—no shot glasses anywhere—and the bartop wasn't cold at all. You would think we would have lifted our faces right away, but probably a full minute passed before that happened. I think I had only counted to five. I heard Agnes say, "Eight. Nine."

"Blow," said Permission.

We blew. Smoke. Rings of smoke.

"You like that one?" Permission asked. "What do you figure it's worth?"

We were the wrong people to ask. We were. God, it makes me squirm to think how pathetic we were, saying, *Do the magic to me. Me. Me. Please.*

We secretly thought Permission doing his magic on us might change everything, like Ma Rainey's magic changed everything for everyone who listened and for Bessie and Louis and Coleman and Trixie and Ed and Clarence and for Janis and for Permission himself.

But I shouldn't speak for Jo about what we thought. That would anger her—and then it would be just fine with her. If she and I had let ourselves, if she hadn't caused her own death nineteen years ago, we could have fallen in love.

And I shouldn't speak for Agnes who has been married to me for nineteen years and with whom I have a beautiful daughter, Rosy. Agnes will let me speak for her anytime, but will always hate me for it later. If we would let ourselves, we could fall in love.

A joke walks into a bar with a man. A man walks into a bar with a heart stuck on a sharp stick. With a beautiful, blindfolded swan. With a hound pulling a hound by its leash. It should add up.

Cascade Lake

Mary and I had not said to our eleven-year-old son Lewis he might not live, had not told his older brother, had not spoken it to each other. In the year after surgeons freed the dark angel sealed behind the window of his skull, we fell out of one way of knowing without knowing yet how we might live now. We had withdrawn from Death her right to be our one truth. We had won, my wife and sons and I, and we should not gloat, we thought. We did not say we thought that. We did not say. Eventually, we touched more than we had ever touched, and broke silence, and talked like people will talk who have raced to a steep falls and have pitched themselves over and, unamazed, surfaced broken and spilled into one another.

On our pre-dawn hike to Cascade Lake in Yellowstone, our bear bells rang in the freezing wind. The bells kept you safe, it was said, from bears with a sense of humor and from bison and moose who love best the stupidest of humans.

In the darkness Lewis quietly laughed and asked, "Whose idea was this?" knowing it was his, and understanding we were lost. He was beyond us on the narrow wrong trail, so when we three reached out for him, we brushed only against each other.

We said his name, said, "Lewis!" the wind stripping the word from our throats.

"*Lewis,*" I said so he and they and God and wind heard. "*Lewis.*"

He said, "I'm here."

A year before, I would have asked, Where? I would have said, You come here right now.

His brother Clark—God forgive us—Clark, Lewis—muttered exactly what I expected: "You prick."

We did not hear Lewis say, "Hey. Choke on it," but Lewis would say that kind of thing, and when he said whatever it is he said then, I thought I heard what I knew I would. It made me feel good, this certainty, as we penetrated the yielding surfaces of a fog-enshrouded marsh and unsteadily sawed our legs through deeper, hellish coldnesses toward more frightening lostness.

"Suckage," said Lewis, and he pivoted right into us, he was that close. "Suckage." He pushed his flashlight under his chin, sending light up through his jaw, making his ears and eyes glow. Red light breathed from his grin, flickered like neon. "Here's where we go," he said, "along here," and pointed to the shallow stream we were already almost walking in, and said, "Watch out for that," but planted his own boot in the smooth glass of a watery black ring where a shadow that swam slingshotted out, a duck, shedding the glistening rank oil of the marsh from its belly and throat. "Ghost!" shouted Lewis, and left us in darkness again, and disappeared behind the falling curtain of stinging rain, the opening wing of night.

An hour earlier, I would have said, You, wait one second, will you? Truth is, I said this now anyway, and I was ignored. Shivering, whispering, Mary said, "Stop him," to Clark who said, "The little prick," but followed the little prick's advice and left us wandering behind, her hand lost in mine, mine in hers.

We took small steps that cracked ice, could hear the wind whip their clothes, and knew the sucking noises of their boots were close, and felt no less lost. We slogged, stumbled, heard Lewis's laughter, laughed, heard Clark's curse, cursed. It seemed like months and more miles and months of this. In Mary's breath I heard the bad solemn verses of diagnoses, the doggerel of a tumor's growth, always named its "progress." I heard the conjured names of the brain's regions and remembered each region's functions and peculiar forms of justice.

One current of violet lifted into a lighter current above it in the fog that chained our waists together in punishing cold dampness. Along the stream the weed stems whispered and the watercress swaying at the surface gasped.

"Look," said Lewis, far ahead of us, the wind and his voice one faint, fading, singing thing. He had come to the lake. He had found Clark.

We heard them slap each other's backs, the way they did. Too rough, we always said, Too rough, but it did no good and, after all, it was a good sound to hear. Where we walked, spirits of fermenting stench closed around us. We stopped, stood in muck and grass and reeds compressed in a giant bed.

"Moose nest," said Mary, her breath close to my face. Her gloved fingers raked my sweatshirt hood back.

"They nest?" I asked.

"They nest."

"Well, Jesus Christ," I said. I pictured giant brittle eggs gently ripped by the velvet racks of cheeping mooselings. "You know *so much*," I said. "You're a genius."

She laughed, said, "Frank, you're an ass."

We should have been able to spark ourselves with such craziness. There should have been no silence that could close back over our delight.

"Hear us?" shouted Clark. "We're here!"

"We're here!" shouted Lewis.

"You sure are," I said, unsure where the hell they were, Mary dragging me forward to the place where their voices had thundered against the skin of water. Strands of crimson stretched across the lake, and within the web new webs churned in menacing whorls. The entire brow of pines on the west rim seemed to ascend as light ascended in the interwoven limbs. On the glistening mud edges of the shallow east rim, violet blades of wave sliced apart the tissues of starlight.

"Small one," I said.

Mary said, "You could throw a rock across it."

We had wanted what we expected. We had. Sixteen years of more love and less loss than others have known had made us as certain and as stupid as all people standing certain at the edges of the stupid places they have blindly followed stupid, certain paths to find. Now, we stood together, one bound, broken, and bound circle. Natural as ever, Lewis nudged us apart, put his arms around our shoulders, said, "Hey, Clark."

And Clark, older, older, knew in an instant what he himself wanted was to be close, and what he expected was to leave us. "The Hug Thing," he said. "I'll pass." This was a way of loving that it seemed right to me he was learning, but I asked, "You sure?"

He said, "I'm—" and he misstepped, and from the slick lip of grass we stood on, he fell headlong into the lake.

As if we were a cape attached to him, we all three fell in hauling him out, and all three stumbled back with him and crashed again in the water and hollered and slosh-hopped and landed apart in our own puddles on the bank.

We sprawled. Silent.

"Suckage," said Lewis, his teeth already rattling.

We took off our down coats and wrung them out, and Clark put his own yellow one on but then mumbled, "Dumb," to himself, and stripped it off and paced and asked, "Now what?"

"We turn blue," said Lewis.

"We turn back," said Mary.

"We make a fire?"

"No matches."

"We wait for the sun?"

"Too long."

Clark shivered. Steam rose from his head. Steaming mud bled from his neck onto his chest. "Goddamngod. God!" he cried. Stunned from the inside out, he panicked, struck himself down on the ground, swung his arms at Mary to warn her away when she came to him.

My compassless, driven, crowded heart failed me. I couldn't act, know, decide. I almost couldn't hear. I might have heard Lewis say, "Help." I might have thought it strange the fearful, exhilarated way he spoke the word. He pointed at the sky where narrow rays plunged through torn clouds and trees and opened light in the shallow bottom of the lake. They would not lift toward us in the hour-long minutes we watched them. Instead, sharp wind that must have been with us all along, sharpened against the ice of our clothes and skin.

"We turn around," I said. And Mary commanded, "*Now*."

"No," said Clark, "I won't. Can't."

"We have no choice," I said.

It will seem impossible that we did what we did next. Even now, spilling our story out like this, I don't believe us.

We listened to Lewis.

Lewis stripped his coat off, pulled his wool cap over Clark's wet hair and whispered to him, "We go in," and said to us, "We go in," and before we could ask, What do you mean? he went.

Up to his waist in half a dozen strides, he said, "Warmer than the air" and lowered his arms in and, almost at the center, dared Clark, who had already followed him there, to go up to his neck.

When Clark whooped, "You little prick!" Mary and I duckwalked our way to him. Mary said, "Goddamn!" and "The water's lovely!" and "Lewis! Hand me the soap." She punched my heart underwater.

Clasped in the sun's talons, a cutthroat broke the warm surface, making rings of warm silence around warmer, wider, slower rings of sound. Lewis said, "Did you hear?" He went under to hear better.

THE COMPLETE HISTORY OF NEW MEXICO

PART II:
THE CIVILIZATION OF THE MESILLA VALLEY

Mr. Belter:

Your footnotes and bibliography are correct. Your spelling is excellent. Except for punctuation and problems with usage, your stepmother has corrected your work throughout. You have not misled me as you intended. Your stepmother has corrected every page of this. That is not allowed.
   MINUS 20 points.

Your photographs do not relate to the history of New Mexico in any way.
   MINUS 10 points.

You cannot give information about yourself and your friends Daniel and Marty and your elderly friends and your family in a research paper about the civilization of New Mexico. I do not believe you should be penalized points for this infraction.

You must tell your teacher the secret locations of the rose mounds. You must bring the shovel to me and the lamps and the clothing of the prostitutes. I will not believe Mr. Rush Bradbridger exists until you introduce me. Are you and your stepmother aware that Edna Kabotie was my sixth-grade teacher? If so, you each must offer an apology to me for trying to take advantage of my emotions. Since you have not provided this information and this personal introduction and this apology, you will receive no credit for supporting evidence.
   MINUS 30 points.

Although you have cheated, lied about facts, left out the very most important supporting evidence, put in excess information, and have provided irrelevant illustrations, you have improved significantly.

I must receive a visit from your father, alone, immediately.

40 of 100 points = F

Mrs. D. Bettersen

The Civilization of the Mesilla Valley

by Charlemagne J. Belter

Mrs. Dorothy Bettersen
Summer School Fifth Grade
June 30 1965

MY OUTLINE

The Introduction
    A) Settlement Jobs
    B) Slave Women
        1) God
        2) golden teeth
        3) good dresses
    C) Civilizing Nuns
    D) The Teenage Boy Problem
    E) Old Lacemakers
        1) secret Spanish words

I. Mule Prostitutes
    A) My Stepmother
    B) Semi Senor
    C) Moor Mules and a picture
        1) lamps
        2) shovels
        3) herbs
    D) Trees
    E) Seven Settlements
        1) Peligro
        2) Dip and Courtesy Pays
        3) Bridle Path
        4) Baby Ducks
        5) Y Limits
        6) Hatch
        7) West of town

II. Rose Mounds
   A) The Progress of Unhappiness
   B) Happiness
   C) Rosa Eglanteria
   D) Mound Building
   E) Bet and Semi
   F) God's Memory and A Gang of Trees and a picture
   G) Sycamores and Moor Mules
   H) The Spanish Hoofprints
   I) The B&A Camera
   J) Corrections

III. Tenders

IV. Madame Edna
   A) Y Limits
   B) Madame Edna Zaldivar Kabotie and a picture
   C) Slave Words
   D) The Marty Expedition

V. Parties
   A) The Signs of the Cross
      1) mica and mustangs and dances
      2) sturgeon and plants and smooth smokes and a picture
      3) Bet

VI. The Seventh Mound
   A) Semi Senor of the Marty Party
   B) The Secret Places and a picture
      1) the seven beautiful cups and the magic stone
   C) Supplications
   D) Urns and Casks
   E) Some Spaniards Go Home

THE CIVILIZATION OF THE MESILLA VALLEY

My Introduction

People wonder where all the Spanish women were when the
Spanish Conquerors and the Spanish Missionaries and the Spanish
Colonists and Armor Repairmen and Blacksmiths and Cooks and
Sheepers and Barbers came. Well the thing is those guys all had
more than one job.

The Conquerors were treasure hunters when they weren't con-
quering. And the Missionaries were teachers and wardens and the
Colonists were farmers or herders and the Barbers did surgery
on the side and the Sheepers were psychologists but they called
them seers and some of the Cooks were skinners or candlemakers
and some of the Blacksmiths were swordmakers too but to be a
swordmaker you had to know your prayers because you prayed
the whole time you made swords. You prayed and forged and hammered and prayed some more and sharpened and polished. The
swordmakers were the holiest ones. This stuff is actually in books
you read about The Coming of the Spaniards and all the Viceroys
and Fryers and Governors. There are not a whole lot of photographs like are supposed to go in here. I have taken some pictures
with my dad's camera and I've put some of them in.

The Spanish Men did a lot of things at the settlements. But who
knew where the women were? You had some Indian women you
would enslave. You would treat them good as examples of how good
you could treat the natives and you would give them golden teeth
even and religion and you would wash them and dress some of
them up and make them have slave children and put some of the
children to work as food testers because there was some poisoning
that went on.

You had a few Civilizing Nuns because that's what nuns did but
they didn't go out of wherever they went. Like if they went into the
mission compound with really high walls and Spanish hens and
vegetable gardens and white adobe buildings and such by a mission

79

church that's where they stayed. With this kind of Civilizing Nun things got out but not much got in. My friend Daniel who was my best friend in all the world and who was a Catholic told me that and he told me the Indians would call the Christians "Christians" if they meant robbers and killers and slavers. He is dead. Daniel is dead. If they meant something else they called them something else.

Indian girl children were brought to the nuns to be civilized and sometimes an Indian boy would be civilized but they didn't civilize the teenage boys because according to I.C. Burns in his book <u>Flesh Made Word</u> "They couldn't."[1]

You had lacemakers who were real real old ladies and some-times they were the swordmakers' mothers and made lace real slow with secret Spanish words sewn in so lacewearing men didn't know they were being called cow dung and goat slobber and salt-peter and a lot worse. The lacemaker ladies who lived almost for-ever because revenge makes you eternally young[2] never wore lace. Never. Lace was always for somebody else.

Mule Prostitutes

The ones that I studied most about were Prostitutes like my stepmother who isn't married to my father. My mother died a long time ago and my father who repairs things couldn't fix how he was which was lonely until he met Bet which is my stepmother's name and short for Elizabeth and what she likes to be called instead of Elizabeth or Beth or Mom. Her name is Elizabeth Ives Celaya and he met her in Hayden's Hardware in June 1963. She is a speech-writer for the Governor of New Mexico a Republican and she says that makes her a prostitute which my Dad says is right and he loves her so I don't argue.

In the Mesilla Valley here you can still go see the places that were civilized with Senor Semi Mendoza who was a cab driver then a school bus driver and then a semi-truck driver and a city bus driver and if he can find his straw hat he will take you to where you can see The Spanish Hoofprints. Like I said I have taken pictures with my dad's black & white because you're going to need them to show you things but the things they show you might not be real clear. You need to look close.

The Conquistadors had horses. The priests and nuns and colonists and all of them didn't. Horses were hard to bring and break and hard to breed because they weren't like the horses today that travel all over and watch a lot of television and eat junk food. My Grandpa in Orla Texas told me that but he is family so he can't be in my Bibliography.

The Prostitutes who had to get around at night had mules called Moor Mules because a slave named Esteban who was a Moor used to use them a lot to lead parties. The mules had lamps on their heads and on their hindends and braided in their tails were herb stems. And they had shovels hanging from the saddleloops. The metal shovels had handles made from Coast Live Oak but the Spaniards called the wood encina and later on Padre Junipero Serra had them planted at every mission because he had a thing about trees and sometimes even before there was a church there he would hang the bells that were going to go into the belltowers

81

onto the branches of the Junipers around there and he would ring those things like crazy until the Indians would want to kill him or be saved.[3] The shovel handles were taken from communion rails in Madrid in Spain. That's what the historian woman Madame Edna Zaldivar Kabotie tells in her book <u>The Roses of the Rio</u>. She knows almost everything about the prostitutes so there must be other books she had to read. No one made Madame Edna write a Bibliography and she doesn't mention the other books. The only other primary source I could find that told about the muleriding prostitutes and their mounds is <u>The Great Basin</u> by Dr.Linnaeus Bentham who doesn't know what he's talking about because his book tells all about them and their roses and their speech lessons and then he says they were legends and not real.

Semi Senor who looks a thousand years old is another source a firsthand and that's supposed to be okay for the term paper. We see him all the time because Bet and my dad watch after him. He doesn't always make a lot of sense but when he does he can make sense of a lot. Semi Senor says roses do not lie and hoofprints do not lie and the amazing speech of the people of the seven settlements do not lie. "El Professor Doctor Benthams should come by here and look" Semi Senor says. He says that history written by people who don't get off their asses is Assxxxx History. I didn't put in quotes there because that is not an exact quote because you can't write out some things without hell to pay and a lot of Spanish was in there and because Semi Senor puts in s all over the place and so you have to put in the s and it doesn't look right and makes me nervous about my grade and so I won't footnote it but I'm going to put it in my Bibliography.

Semi Senor eats jalapenos by the pound and they make his face melt under his eyes and on his chin and under his chin. When I told him I had to write this paper and I needed his help he liked being asked and he agreed to take me and Bet to the rose mounds around Peligro and Dip & Courtesy Pays and Baby Ducks and Bridle Path and Y Limits and Hatch. He took us to The Seventh Mound too. It's up on Highway 70 on the way west out of the Mesilla Valley.

Rose Mounds

There was all kind of Progress that the Conquerors and Colonists and Missionaries brought. They brought cool haircuts and lice combs and dental care and music instruments and painted pictures of El Papa which is what they called God and the Pope too to the settlements of the Mesilla Valley but Semi Senor says there was no happiness until the prostitutes brought that from The Old World to The New World.

The prostitutes were teachers mostly. They taught lessons to the men and some of the women and also some nuns "of a certain persuasion."[4]

They taught good speech to a lot of teenage boys and girls that were going crazy because they were slaves and wanted to get out of town. And they brought a rose called Rosa Eglanteria to The New World which they planted in terraces on mounds of earth thirty or forty feet high. It was a pink rose when they brought it but the dirt here or something turned it red. They did all the mounding and planting and teaching at night because happiness was not exactly legal at that time. People and the official people too knew it was around because you had to be stupid to not see the mounds where the men and women would come and where the prostitutes gave the teenage slaves the free speech lessons. They were trying to help. They were trying to take care of the people because you got to figure you're better off as a slave if you can talk the same language as the slaver and you might be pretty powerful if you could talk the same slaver language even better than the slaver.

They were strong prostitutes you can tell because there is a moat ditch kind of thing about a hundred and fifty yards around every mound. It's where they dug from the earth for the mounds. And in Y Limits and Bridle Path the ditches are about four feet deep. They must've been eight or ten feet in 1609 to 1680 which is about the time this paper tells about.

Seven mounds. Twelve prostitutes in every team. Digging and digging like el lapiz de diablo which means like The Devil's Pencils.[5]

When they weren't digging and planting they wore veils and

midnight blue things so when they were riding in the darkness to one of the mounds to teach people you could see the lamplit mulebehinds and mulefaces staying in the air like headlights do but you couldn't see the prostitutes until they were right on top of you.

I explained that my stepmother Bet is a prostitute who does not like typing that and would not except for love. I didn't explain that she is a Roseologist and cares a whole lot about roses and rose history. Bet went with Semi and me everywhere we went to for this paper. Semi said that was good because you can always use one more person's prayers. And Bet said she was all out of prayers. And Semi said you write this down in your hands or somewheres so you have somethings: Dios tarda pero no olvida.

And Bet said Semi should take his brain medicine that he takes and should speak English so he would make sense and he said that the important thing is that they were looking and Bet said they were going to find Her they were going to find Her by God but she didn't tell me what she meant until later. (This has got nothing to do with anything but my Dad says Semi probably is in mental trouble and Bet and him are the only people on earth looking after him because Semi Junior is who knows where Semi Junior is.)

What Semi said it means is God is late a lot of times but He doesn't forget—Dios tarda pero no olvida.

When you're getting close to the mounds you can smell the rosiness. At all the mounds you have to walk through a grove of Quixote Sycamores that have got their own birthday candle smell and they have got arms that reach up but some of their elbows are low enough they look like they're reaching for each other and for the roses and for something else they want to find. Semi said that when the roses aren't in bloom you can still smell the nectar that goes from the roots to the leaves and to the air where it falls down on the roots in nectar rain. Bet said the bushes smell the way a peachstone would if you tore it out of a fresh peach and left it in a bottle of scotch for 450 years. The roses are grown out of roses that old—450 years—and the ditches and mounds are that old.[6] And the ring of old Sycamores is not a true ring anymore. It's a gang of Sycamore descendants that couldn't move or run away—

A Moor Mule

because of what they are. They're trees. Outside the gang of trees are some of The Spanish Hoofprints that show where the prostitutes' mules were parked that watched the women dig and plant and lift off their veils and bring happiness to the Mesilla Valley. The women had some diseases but not the kind that kill you fast and it was a good thing for them that the Indian people knew some cures and a bad thing that they didn't know all the cures.

They weren't big mules but they were calm you can tell from my hoofprint picture I was going to put in but I didn't because there is another hoofprint I have for later and two hoofprint pictures is stupid. My dad calls his camera his B & A camera. He takes a picture of a thing before he fixes it and then after. He uses black and white film because color doesn't make any difference in a picture of a broken thing and even less once it's put right.

There isn't much of the mules left and that makes people sad.

Semi looked at The Hoofprints and rubbed his eyes to rub away the wet.

Bet looked at them—they don't lead to anywhere—and she rubbed her eyes too and made streaks because she wears too much makeup. And I don't know what she'll do about that because she told me she would type this up for me and even put in Spanish marks and Spanish upsidedown questions sometimes but she said she wouldn't make corrections where she thought I was wrong.

Tenders

Who tends after the mounds is something you'd like to know.
The mounds are not trimmed up. They're not messed up. The
ditches are clean like they're raked by tenders. I explained to Bet
and Semi how the tender people have come here for all the ages.
It's in Mrs. Clute's book <u>The Miracle of Potash</u> where she tells how
no one knows who the tender people are or who they were or how
we'll know them when we see them.

Bet said "Want to meet one?" Semi said "Want to meet one?"
Imagine that.

Madame Edna

In Y Limits which is a few miles south of the sister towns of Dip and Courtesy Pays Semi Senor showed us an unhitched pigeon-peppered trailer off into the Sycamore band around the rose mound they got there.

The trailer was about the size of a bus and about the shape of a lawn grub. It was silver once and Sycamores are kinda gray and so you almost couldn't find it in the gray silverlike light around the Sycamores. This was about 1675 when this mound was made but it could have been 1645. In a book called The Relation of the Troublous Journey of Our Party Gaspar Perez de Villagra Jr. tells about the revolts in 1645 and 1675 but it's confusing what happened when because he jumps all over the place which is why they called Mr. Villagra Jr. "El Chapulin." Grasshopper.

Madame Edna Zaldivar Kabotie kissed Bet and kissed Semi Senor on his face which was old but not as old as hers. He looked at her the same way my dad looks at Bet. You'd have to say he was conquered. People can love the people who conquered them and conquerors can love the people they conquer if they don't make them slaves or kill them or start right off on religion. Madame Edna said "We are together once more. Let us hope. Let us hope! You will acquaint me with this boy's journey and I shall offer assistance." I couldn't hardly believe we were talking to the writer of The Roses of the Rio. But we were. She had a paper map she drew herself of the 7 rose mounds. She had some of the leather faceplates and buttplates the mules wore for the lamps. I strapped on a buttplate and she let me put one of the cloth helmets on. Semi Senor asked her to let me hold the shovel she had.

When it was all on I told her I felt just like a prostitute. Madame Edna called me "A lovely lovely boy" and she swallowed something bad it looked like which made Semi Senor grin but he might have already been grinning. She lifted the helmet off my head and took back the buttplate and shovel and let me interview her for this paper.

I didn't write down much of it.

Rose Mound at Bridle Path

She is related to one of the speech students of one of the prostitutes and you could believe that because of how good she could talk.

It was like this. The prostitutes secretly taught three generations of slave boys and slave girls in seven secret places. That would be maybe a thousand all totaled who could read and who spoke as pretty as Madame Edna. They taught a thousand who taught a thousand who taught a thousand. All of them started up by learning to read the same words:

Alguna vez,
O pensamiento,
serás contento.

Madame Edna read the words to us from an old book from her library. The edge of the pages were redgold. Hearing her was like being poked in your heart and having chile juice poured in. Some day, some day, O troubled breast, Shalt thou find rest.[7] I asked if she knew other people like her in the Mesilla Valley—people who sounded like roses singing.

"I listen for them. I hear them." That's what she said. Her left arm was inside Semi Senor's arm and his was kind of bent out and their fingers were together so their arms either looked like something raveled or unraveled depending on your view.

She said to Bet "Let us hope. I will hear this child we wish to find wherever she is and I will know. Let us hope."

"Marty" Bet said.

"Marty" Semi said.

I didn't know we were looking for Marty until right then. I told about Marty in my last paper which got flunked—my best friend's sister. After Daniel died on the railroad tracks she was a runaway and nobody would ever say anything about her so that meant she was a successful runaway and that made me happy but it turns out my Dad and Bet were looking for her and Semi was looking too and I'm guessing that Madame Edna was listening for Marty to fly overhead like a crow so Madame Edna could just pick her out of the air by a claw or tailfeather.

90

The cat was out of the bag so Bet told me. Semi and Mrs. Orofolo and Mr. Alvarezo and everybody were looking for Marty. They were looking for her from 1963–1965 my dad said that night. He likes popcorn and he can eat it one kernel at a time no problem. He ate a kernel and told about how far they searched and he ate one and told about how many people looked. And I ate most of the popcorn myself and he asked if I missed Daniel and did I know Marty back then when I was in the fourth grade and how much did I remember.

I said I remembered that Daniel was omiscient.

He said what is that.

I said it was a word that Daniel liked and it meant he could see and know everything.

He made me spell it. I said Daniel could find Marty. If he was still here he would.

Parties

The way you decided where to civilize next was that you would get an old slave who had never been out of the Mesilla Valley but said he had been all over everywhere and knew about some places where you could trip your horsehoofs on the chunks of gold and silver everywhere. You would make him lead your party.

And there were Party Rules.

If you didn't find anything you shall kill the guy who was usually an Apache or Comanche or Pawnee you had saved for God.

If you found something neat like mica or mustangs or new dances you shall send a Messenger back to the Governor of where you came from with a wooden cross about the size of your palm. The Messenger shall show the cross so people just know—he wouldn't have to talk or anything.[8]

If you found something like sturgeon or like million-year-old sweet corn or onions growing everywhere and other plants that tasted good or smoked smooth or new slave children you shall send a bigger Messenger back with a bigger cross about the size of your chest. And that way everybody back home would know you were great and still religious.

Sometimes the Messenger shall come back with a cross tall as the front of a barn.

So you've got to imagine what it was like when my dad found Bet. She is the coolest. And she is the reason we didn't leave Hatch after Daniel died because we were packed up and we were tying things to the roof of the Plymouth but then Dad met Bet at the Hayden's Hardware where he was looking for cord and she was looking for car oil.

He said she showed him some knots when he asked Juan and Vicente Fremont behind the counter how to knot cords onto the car and they both said they knew about straps and buckles but not knots and she said what did he need to know.

Knots all night. He practiced them. He showed me. I practiced. They were beautiful knots and that's what connected my Dad and Bet at first and then me that summer.

Twin Towns of Dip & Courtesy Pays

My dad told me he was going to ask Bet to live with him. After that was when I wrote a really complete history paper for English and got the news that I had to go to summer school because I do not do so good at my English classes which are all taught by the same person at my school.

I asked if he asked her.

He said no. He said it was complicated and it involved other people and I thought he meant me but it wasn't just me he wanted to look after.

Million-Year Onions in Sacks

The Seventh Mound

From this mound you can see all the other mounds in the Mesilla Valley. Going to it with Semi and Bet and Madame Edna in Semi's Ford Fairlane at his max speed of 25 I was thinking about how it all figured—the way Daniel and his sister Marty and their dad who was a writer talked. Different.

About where The Splasher Waterpark is on Highway 70 on your way to Lordsburg and Deming is where you're going to find the biggest mound of roses. It's hard to take a picture because there are mining piles and haulers and things in the way that you can't move.

It was an hour or so until night and I found out Semi Senor wasn't very good in his head at night. Like for one thing he said "Have you have a roads Raven?" and was putting his two fists up on either side of his face like he had hold of bars or some big vines or the edges of a book opened up in front of his face. "Eh Raven? Eh Raven?" I asked if he knew a raven somewhere and he said Marty's name then and he looked into the book. And he was reading from the book to her. "¡Oh noche guiaste! ¡Oh, noche amable mas que el alborada!"[9] And you really do have to put things upside down like that when you write something Spanish which says a lot if you ask me. But no book was there and no Marty. I asked Bet did Semi even know Marty. She said "He was the school bus driver once." Well I knew that—we all called him Bus—but did he KNOW Marty was what I was asking.

She said—and it was no answer at all—Semi was a Sundowner because of the mental thing. When the sun went dim it got hard for him to find his way inside his own brain. Bet said Semi was upset about Marty being lost and that's why he was sundowning. Looking into the book that wasn't there but had a story written in it was really confusing him a lot and probably making his sundowning worse.

So I asked the obvious question. If you were prostitutes and you were trying to keep all the places secret where you taught the slave boys and the slave girls then why would you put big mounds up and big tree gangs and roses you could smell a mile away?

Semi said "Spit?" like the way you offer somebody gum and say "Gum?" And he spat on the ground in the place where he had thrown the invisible book which was by San Juan de la Cruz who wrote his best stuff in prison in Toledo.

Madame Edna put her arm around Semi's shoulder and looked down at the spitty book with him. She said I should give Semi the camera—that would help. And she was right. I said she sure knew a lot about Semi Senor and she said she was a Researcher so she researched things other people already searched. Semi Senor looked into the little eyepiece where the thing you picture is the only thing and everything around it isn't there.

I asked my question. If you were prostitutes and you were trying to keep all the places secret—all that. I didn't think anybody heard.

Semi said "If I. If I. If I put seven beautiful cups on the grounds—at night—late at night—and I—I could—I could make you doubt make you believe one magic stones is hiding inside one beautiful cups. Couldn't I? Sometimes I could put no stones under any of the beautiful beautiful cups—or sometimes the simple stones where a magic stones should be. How many times if I if I—how many times—when half the times you refuse to guess—would you guess right the right beautiful cup?"

That is not what he said exactly. He repeated himself the way a broom does in a corner. I didn't write it down but I put it in parts of my head and I've brought out most of it from one part I think.

The thing is the prostitutes used only one mound at a time and it was night. It was like one or two in the morning when they gave the lessons which probably were not easy. I could remember adventuring all over the place with my friend Daniel. He could talk some Spaniard. We were always searching out secret people and secret places. What good did that do Daniel? He couldn't find a place to hide from his dad ever who he loved and who seemed like he loved Daniel but couldn't have loved him really.

One of the missionaries who unconverted himself got lost when he was escaping the settlement and he wrote things down that he wanted to tell or pray—but not a lot of them.

The dirt, the water of the rivers, the red beetles in the flesh of the agave taste of blood. My clothing gone, my shame unshed. God answers. God does not answer. There is no wrong that lasts forever, and no happiness that cannot end.[10]

I said "We're never going to find Marty are we?"
Semi looked at me through the camera. "Have faith" he said.
"We have searched for a very long time." Madame Edna touched the back of his head with both her hands and she stopped touching and then patted his hair and stood close.
Semi said slow and by memory and this is what he said exact— his mouth moved under the camera so he was like God in a God mask—he said "Everythings we search for searches for us forever. Everythings that was one things has been changed into manything. Everythings that was manything has been changed into one things." And Semi said "Put it in your footnotes"[11] because it's the words Gaspar Perez de Villagra Jr. said that Don Juan de Onate said to his chief cook who said it to his butcher who had a son who had a grand greatson who was the Royal Historian a lot later after the 17th Century but I can't find it in any books anywhere including the old ones but I knew I should still put it in.
There's no water around the seventh mound. You've got to imagine that the speech students carried water there—the price they paid for the lessons. That's something you can read about in The Roses of the Rio:

It is thought that the children brought water in clay urns made expressly for this purpose by The Old Ones. There is an urn in the possession of the Mesilla Valley novelist Mr. Rush Bradbridger, the throat of which resembles the fountain-like sepals of a rosebud. The concave base has a small headband of woven maguey fiber inside. This urn holds approximately six and one half gallons of liquid when it is full. It is the sole urn of its kind. It has not been authenticated by experts.[12]

No one has a bucket or urn to prove anything. It makes sense that they could be big urns if somebody ever finds more of them because slaving can make you ready to carry anything. You look at The Stone Hinge. You look at The Pyramids. Hoover Dam.

Look at the Sycamores. The Sycamore seedlings came in casks the size of A bombs.

When he put the camera away Semi sundowned again. He couldn't just hold it against his eye the whole time we walked around in the Sycamore circle. Twelve old Sycamores and maybe twenty or so around them. Madame Edna said we would not cross the ditch to the mound. It would not be proper.

Semi who wanted to cross over cried like a baby and said "Lemony" to his feet in order to make them go around with us under the Sycamores. "Lemony. Lemony." Just crying at them and commanding them to go. His feet.

It was time for the Spaniards to go home when the civilizing was done. After 71 years in New Mexico a lot of them got back on their horses and wagons to go south but they left their mothers and their nuns and they kept the lacemakers here but they made them send all the lace they ever made back to The Old World. There is not much of it around here except for what Mr. Rush Bradbridger has who keeps it for himself and I'm with Bet about that—she says he should be arrested. There's a lot of that lace in Spain in a lace museum there but nobody will show it to you because there's so many bad words laced into most of it.

The Spanish Hoofprints

Some of the Spaniard men who never got lucky finding the prostitutes under the beautiful cups guessed right one night. Most of their buddies had gone back to The Old World that year so the ones left had nothing to do but look for prostitutes. They found them at The Seventh Mound.

It was around late May. Or June. 1680. Madame Edna wrote about it.

> The Rosa Eglanteria upon the mound would have been
> in their second and last cycle of blooming, a fragrant
> pool of fallen petals at their bases, the blossoms smaller
> than in the first cycle, but in wider profusion.[13]

Thirty or forty children sat around—the Sycamores were about the right size to lean against.

> Alguna vez,
> O pensamiento,
> serás contento.
> Si amor cruel
> me hace guerra,
> seis pies de tierra
> podrán más que él:
> allí sin él
> y sin tormento,
> serás contento.

The mules were drawing warnings in the dirt with their hoofs and pointing. It was night but their lamps were just put out so they were still seeing spots but they weren't afraid of the dark. The prostitutes were helping the children recite. What they recited was Old Spanish and wasn't this kind of New Spanish but there isn't much of the Old around to look at. Some of it is in the lace in the lace museum in Madrid. Bet said I should put the whole thing in somewhere but she said it had to be a footnote and it wouldn't count for a real page of my report but that doesn't matter because my report is longer than I planned anyway.

Lo no alconzado
en esta vida,
ella perdida
será hallado
y sin cuidado
del mal que siento,
serás contento.

The children could recite all of it and that's why I put all of it in.

There could have been a full moon or extra stars. Who knows. When the soldiers—probably fifteen or twenty of them—found them and murdered the prostitutes and the children they threw the heads in the ditch and they rode their horses around and around in the ditch like they were riding inside a tornado. Probably hair and bone and golden teeth in there. You can see the hoofprints. They look like a million gray snake scales. None of the other six mounds have hoofprints in the ditch moats. They only have the hoofprints of the prostitutes's mules inside the Sycamore groves.

The soldiers didn't kill the mules or even hurt them.

The Spanish who stayed after that and the ones who left lost all the happiness. It changes everything when you lose somebody and you can't find him and make right what went wrong. The land in New Mexico is dry and hundreds of years of sadness just sets on top of it like rain. The vapor off it waves and then the waves reflect up in the sky and the sky waves too. If there's dust in the air at sunset there's a red tide before it all goes away. Everybody who doesn't know any better thinks it's pretty which it is but not like they think.

The bodies and the heads got buried under The Seventh Mound by the Indian People who had to do the burying in secret at night. The Moor Mules pointed their heads or maybe their hindends at the holes and that made some light.

Behind This Stuff Is The Seventh Mound

They were surprised when a few of the lacemakers brought little pieces of lace with the words "Rogad por nosotros" on them. Semi says he doesn't know what it means but he does. You can't tell everything. You shouldn't. I'm not so stupid I think there's any real place called Y Limits or Bridle Path or Baby Ducks or Dip. Bet said if I put in the real names of the places she would change them. She was going to correct them so they would be wrong even though she promised she wouldn't correct anything. She said that isn't what she promised. So I named the places that are really real with signs like Dip and Y Limits that are really everywhere along the road but you're never going to find a place that is that place which is a shame and also a good thing. "Pray for us" is every-place. "Rogad por nosotros" is a neck tattoo you see all over on gangnecks and it's on Cadillac and Oldsmobile bumpers even.

Everybody was surprised when one of the civilizing nuns came and helped them bury the bodies and put the mound dirt back and then the roses. She stayed out of the nun place after that. She probably wasn't allowed back in Bet says. And she married an Indian guy but nobody knows who he was because you didn't have a US Census that was any good then. And her mule had lamps on its face and hindend and a shovel hanging from a saddleloop. And she wove dried cilantro into the tail. And she and the Indian guy had babies everybody called mestizoninas which are a kind of small weed with gold flowers or the name of the dark nuts on encinas or the children roses that come from the hips of roses. Or something else. The nun was the mother of the mother of the mother of the mother of the mother of the mother of Madame Edna who it turns out was a tender person and the grandmother of Daniel and Marty.[14]

You might be an old tree in a small grove but you don't think you are or know. And some of the seeds from the grove take off—way far off—and some just die on the ground—but some of them stay around and they grow in the same circle the way Semi Senor and Madame Edna did for probably eighty years but they didn't hardly recognize each other and didn't know why they would love each other like they do. Bet says that's history for you and she told me to write it down and she says it's a shame the rules don't let you quote your own parents because then you can't put in your Bibliography the people you can count on most. And she said I better put in the whole poem in English that the children recited.[15]

Mound Moat

My Conclusion

We walked back to Madame Edna's trailer. Semi had some problems moving around in his own brain because his voice gave out. Bet and Madame Edna helped him. They said "Lemony Lemony" to his feet.

I said I wished Daniel was with us.

I said Daniel could find Marty.

Nobody was saying anything. I said Marty would be about 10 years old now.

Bet asked Madame Edna "Will we keep searching?"

Madame Edna said "No. No. It is over." And she held onto Semi's shoulder and walked with him and asked Bet and me if the two of them would be lost too.

Bet made a vow. She said she and my dad and me would take care of Madame Edna and Senor Semi all their lives no matter what. And that meant to me my dad had asked Bet to move in and have one child which was me and have two real old ones and she was saying yes and I knew it before he did.

We did take care of them.

But Madame Edna died one week later. One week is all it took and at her funeral Semi Senor looked through my dad's camera and cried real hard behind it. And she was buried near The Seventh Mound.

FOOTNOTES

[1]I.C. Burns Flesh Made Word pgs. 22–23.

[2]Geronimo The Autobiography of Geronimo pgs. 503–503.

[3]Padre Miguel Pieras Beneath the Boughs pgs. xi.–xii.

[4]Lea K. Muggenberg Clute The Miracle of Potash pg. 9.

[5]Interview with Semi Mendoza on April 31 1965.

[6]Madame Edna Zaldivar Kabotie The Roses of the Rio pg. 847.

[7]Cristóbal de Casillejo The Poems of Cristóbal de Casillejo translated by Henry Wadsworth Longfellow pg. 1.

[8]Juan Crespi Unedo Summerwood pgs. 6–7.

[9]San Juan de la Cruz It Was the Darkest Night translated by E.Z. Kabotie pg. 80.

[10]Fray Agapito Solomon Hernan Luna The Supplications of Fray Agapito Solomon Hernan Luna translated by Bunnie L. Luna Goldensmyth.

[11]Interview with Semi Mendoza on April 31 1965.

[12]Madame Edna Zaldivar Kabotie The Roses of the Rio pgs. 31.

[13]Ibid. pg. 847.

[14]Ibid. pg. 911.

[51]Some Day

Some day, some day,
O, troubled breast,
Shalt thou find rest.
If Love in thee
To grief give birth,
Six feet of earth
Can more than he;
There calm and free,
And unoppressed,
Shalt thou find rest.
The unattained
In life at last,
When life is passed,
Shall all be gained;
And no more pained,
No more distressed,
Shalt thou find rest.

BIBLIOGRAPHY

Linnaeus Bentham. The Great Basin. Baroque Oklahoma: Dorotea Inc. 1953.

I.C. Burns. Flesh Made Word. Dixon: JMJ and Co. 1955.

Cristóbal de Casillejo trans. Henry Wadsworth Longfellow. The Poems of Cristóbal de Casillejo. Banner Alabama: Naranja Press 1934.

Geronimo. The Autobiography of Geronimo. Prescott Arizona: Curtis Publications 1909.

Fray Agapito Solomon Hernan Luna trans. Bunnie Luna Goldensmyth. The Supplications of Fray Agapito Solomon Hernan Luna. Comienzo New Mexico: Comienzo Community College 1944.

Madame Edna Zaldivar Kabotie The Roses of the Rio. Cid Illinois: Carmelite University Press 1930.

Patrick Secreto Lamb. Seers of the Southwest. Las Almas: DAAC & Co. 1963.

Semi Mendoza. Interview with Semi Mendoza. Charlemagne J. Belter 1965.

Padre Miguel Pieras. Beneath the Boughs. San Diego: Estudios Franciscanos 1949.

San Juan de la Cruz trans.Madame Edna Zaldivar Kabotie. It Was the Darkest Night. Cid Illinois: Carmelite University Press 1936.

Juan Crespí Unedo. Summerwood. Finches New Mexico: Apostolic College de Propaganda Fide 1911.

Gaspar Perez de Villagra Jr. trans. Lysander Hayes. The Troublous Journey of Our Party. Chicago: Urcen Books 1960.

The Rhino in the Barn

for Emily Jean

I was twelve when the two great halves of the fiberglass rhino were sealed, leaving only a slight scar, an unbroken line from spine to tail to belly to the tip of its horn. My father stood under it. "Clara, take the picture," he said, inflated by his accomplishment, though not enlarged enough to touch the belly of the rhino with his upraised hand. Frank, my younger brother, said, "Jesus . . ." and he was not even slapped as he would normally have been for this sacrilege.

Mother, her face deeply flushed, the face of a tuberculin, breathed in only a little, but also seemed inflated. "Take another picture," she said, and she and my father and Frank stood together at the front of the rhino. I moved back to get the creature's entire head above them in the picture, but by the time I was ready to shoot, my mother had deflated again, and she looked frailer than ever.

The next day Father and I drove to what he called "the biggest Esso in the city of St. Louis" to tell the Esso man his rhino was ready. As they talked, I tried to picture the big rhino standing astride the roof of the filling-station garage. But the creature was at least as tall as that building and, though I knew about the lightness of fiberglass, I thought the rhino must be more weight than that roof could bear.

Their uncivil bargaining ended and Father, a tall man, looked down at the short, muscular Esso man. He asked, "What color?"

The Esso man said a little stiffly, "Rhino color, I guess. Just paint it rhino."

We lived in a part of southern Illinois where the soil is always pregnant, but our particular farm was given to difficult and often unsuccessful births. The stretch of land that Father inherited from his father was misfarmed by every generation for over seventy-five years and was gray, unwilling soil. There are few hills of any great height in that hilly part of Illinois, but our land formed a kind of L, closing itself against a steep, rocky hill that in rain always sloughed one of its coats of rock onto the farmland. We grew horseradishes to sell; Mother maintained a vegetable garden before her illness; and we kept chickens and pigs enough to slaughter when we needed. But Father was proud to say, "A man with imagination doesn't have to be only a farmer." He taught himself carpentry, and he built storage sheds and barns and even added rooms to people's houses for a reasonable price.

When Mother first became ill, he built a really fine garage behind our house and did tractor repairs there. Then, a man in Cahokia told him about fiberglass and the future of fiberglass, and it seemed a natural next step for him to close his tractor shop and use it as a place to learn about the marvelous properties of that amazing fiber.

Father studied and studied and experimented and made molds of everything. He made lawn-boy molds and bathtub molds, and he was doing very well with those when he discovered the market for drugstore signs and storefront dummies.

Mother was diagnosed as having tuberculosis. She spent nearly half of the following year in the sanitarium. When she was out for a weekend, we sometimes took drives to Alton and Mitchell and St. Louis to see the various members of my father's fiberglass zoo. At Alma's Maternity Shop in Mitchell we saw the six-foot infant in a crib rigged to rock back and forth. Father explained how easily he set that rocking up; how the crib was one of his tubs modified a little. It didn't look at all like a tub.

Mother asked Frank and me if it looked like a tub to us.

I said, "Uhn-uh," because it really didn't.

Frank, two years younger than I but always the wise guy, said, "Big deal."

Mother looked hurt. She said, "Don't slouch, Franklin."

And Frank sat up straight in the car seat all the way to St. Louis where we saw the black bull at the Black Bull Steak House, then the bear standing up and holding a marquee at the Bayer Theatre, and a few more creatures, including a kangaroo on skates and a horse with wings, all just slightly larger than their real size.

Father had never made a creature more perfect in every detail than the rhino. By placing cables in the mold, he even achieved the texture of the rhino's skin. In size, also, he had never gone so far: the rhino was magnified better than five times.

In our car at the Esso station, he and I talked about the creature. The zookeeper at the St. Louis Zoo had told him rhinos had pleasant personalities but that they didn't travel well. He and I discussed that, what that could possibly mean in understanding rhinos.

On the way back to our farm and the unpainted rhino, I asked Father what color the color rhino was. His smile entirely bared his gums. "Yellow," he said. He giggled at that. He affectionately knocked me at the back of the neck. "With an orange horn!" he said.

Coming around the hill to our farm, we saw Mother and Frank arguing about something. "If that boy's bothering your mother about a bike again . . ." Father began, but, seeing the rhino at beagle-like attention watching our home, he forgot what he had meant to say.

At supper, Mother wanted to know what the Esso man said. I said, "He wants the rhino to be rhino-colored, but—"

Father interrupted, "But the color's a secret between Clara and me."

Mother pretended she was angry. Later, she said, "I won't tempt you, Clara."

In the evening we drove Mother back to the sanitarium. We kissed her good-bye and hurried out of the terrible-smelling place to the car where Father told Frank to sit up front with him. He put his arm around Frank. "No bike," he said. "But. If Clara's agreeable to it, we'll let you in on a secret."

"You won't tell?" I asked.

"Am I stupid or something?" said Frank. So we told him.

The next weekend Mother was too ill to come home, so in the afternoons we went to visit her at the san, where the speckled tile floors were cold and the walls were a color my father called "Not Green."

Suffering the extremest form of exhaustion, Mother spoke little. We had brought her maraschino cherries, her favorite food, and we talked about that. The narrow jar, red-lacquered lid, good juice.

We had more awkward conversation with her, Frank asking—at the end of the longest of several uncomfortable silent pauses—"Are you going to die . . . or what?" He cried with such angry loudness we didn't even try to stop him. When he had finished, Mother unfolded her arms, tapped her fingers on his chest just over his heart. She handed him over to my father.

We teased her about our secret. We told her there was one coat of paint now on the rhino. A coat of one color on the body. A coat of another color on the horn. Going along with our teasing, Mother pleaded to know what color. "You'll see," we said, "you'll see."

"That's okay," she said. "Frank will tell me."

Frank brightened. "Who? Me?" he asked. For a moment, we could tell he was going to give it away. But Mother's face was beaming, and he must have discovered in it the importance of keeping a secret until keeping the secret becomes the gift. For us, anyway, the secret became a prized possession, as Father must have known it would when he first gave it to Frank and me.

It was early evening again before Father and Frank and I arrived home. "Hats look good," said Father, referring to the verdant aboveground vegetation of the horseradish plants. Before we came to the house, he stopped the car. He bent to the ground to pull one of the radishes with its odd skull just above the earth. The long root was miserably thin and pliable, the way he had taught us the worst roots always were. It had a rotten smell that displaced all the other pleasant smells of the spring.

Frank said, "Bad season," echoing perfectly even the inflections in Father's way of saying that.

"This don't mean a bad season," Father said, tearing the hat from the root.

"We can pull another one," I said. I took Father's arm, but he pulled away. He handed me the root.

"We'll pull another in a week or so." He wiped his hands on his back pants pockets. "Take that and feed it to the rhino."

Leaving him at the edge of the field, we ran to the place where the rhino stood, and we pretended. We offered it the root. "Here . . . here . . ." we said. Its giant horns were illuminated by the last of the sunlight; its fleshy eyelids cast shadows at the corners of its eyes; and, for a moment, we almost expected it to bow its head to take the horseradish.

In the summer, to recover from the crop loss, Father sold a corner of the land and he put the last coat of bright yellow paint on the rhino in order to sell it now to the very impatient Esso man. Because no one he knew could lend Father a truck big enough to bring the rhino to the Esso man, we drove to St. Louis, without the rhino, to visit the filling station. The Esso man said he only had a tow truck.

"Maybe you don't want that rhino?" said Father, a little angry at the Esso man's casualness about the creature. When the Esso man didn't answer, Father asked, "You backing out? Is that it?"

The Esso man wanted to know, "This rhino—how big is he?"

Father said, "It's a *she*, mister." That was the first Frank and I had heard of the rhino's sex; we had thought of her all along as an it. Following the man as he went to pump gas for a customer, Father said, "She's almost two stories. Has enough belly to hold a Rambler." He made an embracing gesture, and said, "You can't even hardly hug your arms all the way around her legs."

"What?" said the man. As Father told him more about the rhino, the man shook his head and repeated, "What? What?" When Frank giggled at the Esso man's head-scratching, Father made us get back in the car.

Both of us in the passenger seat, window down, we couldn't clearly hear anything but the Esso man's single repeated question. We saw Father take the curved pump nozzle and turn it up like a horn and pass his fingers over it and hand it, like a trophy, to the man. He followed the man into the station garage. A few minutes later he slammed the car door after him. "Let's go to the san," he said.

On the car radio tuned to an East St. Louis station he liked, we heard someone singing, "Get your hand on the dollar, get your mind on another town," and Father said, quietly but with strange intensity, "Who is that?"

At the san, Mother seemed almost happy about the news that the rhino was not sold. "No sir!" said Father, encouraged by her reaction. "That's one Esso the rhino is never going to ride!" He flexed his shoulders as if to relax them, but I recognized that gesture as something Father did at happy times. During my mother's illness, I began also to recognize that in my father's hands and his broad back, in my father's happiness, was a fragile strength, like moth wing, capable of great and continuous exertion, but able to be broken with a breath.

He sang her a bit of the song. She asked him to sing more. "That's Henry Brown and Edith Johnson," she said.

Mother did not get better. She had not been able to visit home for many months when, in October, Father warned us she might not be able to return home again. Frank and I often talked about it on our way home from school; about how she half whispered and half rasped; about how she trembled when she held us.

"And the smell. Do you smell it?" he said.

"Her breath," I said. "Her insides aren't right."

"That's TB," he said authoritatively.

I said, "It's just when your insides aren't right your breath gets bad."

He asked, "Is she going to die?" It would be impossible to calculate how many times he asked that, or how many times Father or I explained that she was too weak to live on the farm but much too strong to die.

He asked, "Well, are we going to tell her what color the rhino is?"

"I don't know, Frank." I asked, "Are we?"

Frank said, "Not me! I'm not!"

As we came around the rocky hill to the farm, we could see the rhino looking out over our land and beyond our land to Missouri and Kansas and farther. Climbing a ladder to her back, Father hollered hello to us. We helped him wash her and towel her dry, then

Father put a blanket on her back and sat us there. "To the Alps!" he said and shouted up to us, "Ride low! Ride low!" We survived whistling storms and crashing avalanches and the lightning that clapped from Father's hands and, finally, a terrifying descent out of the mountains before we came down the ladder again and went inside to eat dinner.

The next morning after breakfast, Father asked Frank to get three persimmons and bring them back. He cut his first and then Frank's and then mine, but at the heart of every seed was the shape of a spoon. "A bad winter," he said.

In the weeks that followed, Father worked late each night and was back to work very early each day. He sold a horse-size bird with a moveable beak to a hardware store in Alton. In St. Louis he sold a bear to a clothing store. It was just like the Bayer Theatre bear except that it had a brown suit and red vest and redder tie put on it when we took Mother to see it.

Until he bought all the lumber, we had thought Father's recent sales were to prepare for the winter. But they were not.

It took him all of November to build the barn around the rhino. My aunt Roberta's husband helped, and my mother's older brother Richard. My aunt Rachel—we called her Aunt Oar—was there every day, and she told us stories about our mother, already using the past tense.

They built a giant, noble barn. They also built an awning to cover the rhino's head, which stuck out of the west wall. But we agreed the awning looked too much like some ridiculous bonnet. So Father and Richard built a windowed box to cover the rhino's whole head; but when Father fit this to the rhino at the neck, it looked like a kind of silly armor. Though the box had been expensive to make, Father could not bear the head armor, and he removed it within the week.

The winter that came was a winter that Father said would bury even the Alps. We were lucky to have a rhino with us, he said, or we'd never make it through. In the evenings, he would suddenly rise from the dinner table or stop working at a sketch for a fiberglass animal and go, without his coat, to the rhino in the barn.

Before we would leave to see Mother, he would take us to the barn, close the door behind us, and say, "Take a look, will you?" Her legs formed such extraordinary columns at the walls and, high above us, her stark yellow underside, a chandelier of teats, formed such a strange ceiling, that she transformed the barn into a palace. "She *does* have a pleasant personality, don't you think?" he would say. "She should have had a longer tail."

"No," I always told him, "This tail's enough. See," and we inspected the tail and the big hinge that attached it to the rhino.

Frank would say nothing about the rhino's tail. In these trips to the barn he became silent and nervous and would speak only to say, "Are we leaving now?" When the two of us were alone, Frank asked, "Is he—okay?"

"Frank!" I answered, "He's unhappy. But he's okay, Frank. He's okay." I don't remember if it ever assured either of us.

On the coldest winter mornings we went outside to study the rhino's head and her brilliant orange horns that sparkled in the sunlight reflected from the snowdrifts around us and the snow on the roof of the barn. "Rhino," Father said. "Now that's a perfect name." I had wanted once to name her, to call her Millicent the Rhino or Hanibella the Rhino, but Father pouted about that. He spoke very little to me for the rest of the day and that, only that odd silence, frightened me. That weekend he told Frank and me, "You can't name animals. It's an insult. God gave man the name Adam, and Adam gave animal the name Rhino and that's enough." I remember he tapped my chest in that same way Mother had tapped Frank's chest, and he said, "Clara. I think Hanibella is a great name. But not for a rhino."

Mother contracted pneumonia that winter and became gravely ill. Because in that time it was believed that fresh air was a possible cure for tuberculins, the san was kept cool and the patients were not given more than one blanket at night. When we saw her she was so frail that to speak exhausted her. I became very good at talking without pause to entertain her, and it made me proud to see how my rambling entertained even Father.

As I grew more extroverted, Frank seemed to slowly implode. Teasing, Father would ask Mother, "Has Frank told you the color yet?" and laugh and put his large hand on Frank's shoulder and say, "Our secret!"

"Don't," Frank said, trying to remove the weighty thing from him. Even Mother must have recognized his fear; Father, who could read persimmons right and read the hats of plants, and design fiberglass molds like no one else, did not realize.

He had not perceived the severity of Mother's illness either. In early February, the month I became sixteen, Mother died. At the funeral, Uncle Richard and his wife asked Frank if he would like to come to live for a short while with them in New Mexico, and Frank pleaded for permission to go with them.

Another bad season followed. Father and I harvested little and could not sell what we harvested because the other horseradish farmers produced so plentifully. Father constructed molds, but could not buy the materials for fiberglass. To pay the last medical bills and the funeral costs, he sold the entire bottom leg of the land, including the farmhouse, to the city for what later became a dumpyard.

When Frank returned, the three of us moved into the rhino's barn.

Now it seems strange that we should have lived so happily there. But we did. It was not odd to us at all, living under the rhino. Father had made her so solid, so permanent was her rhino smile and the sharpness and strength of her horns that at night she seemed almost to lay her great, warm strength over us. I commuted to St. Louis for a job selling cosmetics.

Father had plans to repaint her and to construct a rhino mate. Frank and I and Father pretended the rhino always charged and gored her hunters. The rhino's horns, we decided, were magic: one more magic than the other, but one's magic depending on the other's. The lesser horn could make you pretty, but you needed the greater horn to make you pure. The greater horn could make you happy, but only the lesser horn could bring you joy.

We have kept the barn and the land it is built on. Father lives with me in Mitchell not far from the clothing-store bear. Frank, who has, like me, lived too much of his adult life alone, plans to be married next month in Las Almas, New Mexico.

A year ago, thirteen years after our mother's death, Frank and I returned to check on the rhino. As we drove around the rocky hill surrounded by the dumpyard, we noticed immediately that the head of the rhino was missing. "Someone's taken it," Frank said.

"No," I said. "They couldn't. It's too big."

We opened the barn doors. All the furniture was in place, all the lamps and tables, the empty narrow maraschino jars that we collected. But the rhino was gone. It was not even clear where her feet stood. "She was lighter than we thought," he said.

I felt the tiles. Ghosts were in the tiles and walls and roof where her back had been, her massive sides, her hoofs, her neck, her tail.

Frank said, "It must have been one heck of a job. It'd almost have been easier to take the barn down from around her than to take her apart and out of the barn."

Frank and I still speculate about where the rhino went. When it comes up, I always remember how on the day of the funeral Frank talked to our mother in the car as if she was still there and we were only taking her back to the san. He said, "It was yellow. Bright yellow!" I sat next to him, pretending she was there, too. I felt certain that the rhino was not stolen at all. I could picture her running wildly around my family's farmland, goring the wind with her greater horn to become small enough to leave the barn through a keyhole; goring the wind with her lesser horn to grow giant once more.

Maraschinos

In the grocery store an old friend asked, "It's your anniversary, right, Frank?"

"Twenty-sixth," I said. Down a long tunnel inside me, I found myself asking, "Has it been that long, Ma?" My wedding day in 1975 and my mother's death in 1961 live impossibly in the same body of memory.

I'm ballroom dancing because it's my wedding day and Mary says I have to. I couldn't buy her much of a ring. We can't start out right. I don't make much of an impression and I never did. But all these people, who have traveled so far from Illinois, who I hardly know, but who love her so much—they all love me now and all at once.

People give me a second look they never gave me before.

I'm dancing. I'm out here giving it my best, which is pretty bad.

I'm bleeding. I've got on a bandage the size of my entire chest, thick as a catcher's apron, and I'm bleeding through it.

Two months ago I had a benign tumor taken out of my chest. Had a ginseng-like root on it right through the chest wall over my heart, and it was putting a net of roots around my heart. The tumor came out: to make a long story short—it was a mess. The incisions got infected. Had to be reopened, restitched into an X Marks The Spot thing.

I can't lean over—I'm tall and it's hard to remember to not lean down to talk to the tiny old women I'm dancing with. I can't look up or down or turn my neck and head right or left too fast—hard not to do that on my wedding day with people joking and calling out, "Where'd he learn to dance?" and to my wife, "He's a keeper," or "Are you sure he is?" or "He spilled on himself, looks like." If I raise my arms too fast or don't lower them slow, if I sway or I look or turn or lean like I said, the incisions open and some blood leaks. There is a dribble of red on the front of my white shirt. I tell people who ask me that it's because I spilled on myself with a jar of maraschino cherries.

And what happens with everybody is the same thing. Everybody wants to talk about Ma. Everybody wants to tap me on the X.

Aunt Dee, who works as an auditor for the IRS, who has the elegance to be able to smoke with a long cigarette holder and pull it off, wants to talk about Ma. Leads me to the dance floor, says, "It's a waltz, dear," as if to be kind, to remind me it's no big deal since it's not a job interview, not another hospital bill, not a dance with the IRS. "Frank, your mother was *the* dancer," she says. "The class act. When I miss her, I picture her dancing." Fourteen years after Ma's death, and she's on everybody's mind.

When she was dying they all came to her room and brought laughter and brought a hi-fi, too, and played music. Chubby Checkers! They did The Twist but it looked a lot like The Hokey Pokey—they were that generation. It was like a wedding in there. And so much attention was lavished on Clara and me that Ma seemed hardly there. Clara told me afterwards that I should not take it so personally when everyone said to her that she had to be the "strong one now."

Aunt Dee laughs and says, *"You're* not much of a dancer, *are* you?"

Well, no, I would say but saying that would require dancing and talking at the same time.

"You are dear to me," says Aunt Dee, "and I can tell that you hardly know how much, and that's all right, it's all right."

And then she pats my heart right on the X.

When we're done dancing I see her wipe her hand on a napkin at the table where Dad sits with my sister Clara and with Aunt Rachel who has always made people call her "R," but who says "Oar" in her Kentucky accent. She is pointing at me, marking me for the next dance. Dad's hands are stuck in his back pockets. He has tails on his shiny rented coat, and his jade bowtie is huge as the gullet on a lizard ready to mate. So excited. He's looking right at me and I've seen that love there every hour of my life but now that happiness, well, I have to move my head to look again and I have to wave at him, and that opens the X and causes leakage. I press the bandage so it will absorb the blood, and maybe not spread more syrupy redness over my shirt. I should have brought extra bandages.

Aunt Oar claims me, her hands gripping my arms like I'm a posthole digger. She says, "Your bride's pertiest I ever saw. I'm gonna be rough with you now," and she polka-pivots me so violently to the left my whole chest feels birdshot. "I'm goin to give up a toast," she says, and she has an industrial bosom that does not care at all about getting stained against my shirt. "I'm toastin' your mother in a little bit of a while. It ain't the right occasion and I ain't the right person for it, but just you watch me."

I am not making this up. My ma's picture must be on the table napkins. Her name must be written out in electrical tape on my back.

After the polka, Aunt Oar pats me on the X.

No one except Mary knows about the surgery, the bandages, any of it. So? So. What is the instinct that people have for tapping you where your blood wants out?

I watch Aunt Oar. I have stained her good, and she doesn't care. She sits back down with her brother Richard and her sister Roberta who is next in line to dance with me. Aunt Oar's voice is loud. I can hear her say, "Jesusgod! Look at me!" showing herself, like having people looking at her big red-stained breasts is the best thing that ever happened to her.

And here is no surprise: Roberta pats me on my X.

Maybe people have to touch a stain because it makes them self-conscious. If it's a big Rorschach-type stain, maybe patting it is just a way of asking a man like me, "What does this mean?" I don't usually draw attention. Inside me is pretty much the only place I ever traveled and where I have mostly lived my life until Mary.

And after Roberta, Mary's mother pats the X. She asks, "Should we get you a new shirt, hon?" She is both very smart and very trusting, and her daughter is, and my ma was.

Clara and Dad and I made promises to Ma we could not keep. She saw right through them. She believed them.

Mary cuts in. I try to dance with her but she says, "That's okay," and simply sways with me. In the center of the dance floor, swaying, I don't think we look too bad. She wants to know if I'm okay. "Does it hurt?" We have talked about Ma many times, but that isn't what she means.

We joke about how much blood will be on our sheets after our honeymoon night. Her laughter could be my own. Her cheek is against mine. It's in the movies all the time, the cheek thing, and there is never blood, I notice. With her there is no reaching too far beyond me or too far into me to bring her near me like it seems I have to do with everyone else on the planet. How did she find me? She had to be inside me, everywhere around me. How did I find her? She was already there.

By now, there have been a dozen or more people batting the X. I'm glad the band has taken a break. I'm definitely ready to sit down, but Clara tells the band they have to play one more, and she brings everybody, including the little children, there onto the floor. She's the big sister. She thinks she has rank. When she first met Mary she said, in front of her, "I'm not going to be able to have my way with this one." And to Mary, "You're going to be good for both of us." And that is true.

Clara dances worse than me. I try swaying, but she lets me know it's not an option. I tell her, "You should learn how to dance."

"How?" she asks.

"Get married," I say. "See how good *I* dance now?"

"Your shirt is a mess."

"Spilled." Thinking she might appreciate my excuse, I say, "Maraschinos."

She says, "Look out for Aunt Oar. She's going to make a toast. About our mother—I couldn't talk her out of it."

"Why haven't you gotten married?" I ask her. We look at our feet, which will not make a box or even a triangle.

"I'm going to have to get out more," she says, swaying by rocking on her pink high heels, watching me sway not at all in rhythm with her. She asks, "Do you remember the barn? Illinois. The giant gas-station rhino?"

"It was the best thing, wasn't it?" Clara says.

"I don't know."

I'm always saying something to you, Ma, trying to finish saying something. I go to you inside me, I don't know why, fourteen years after your death. You must wonder about me.

Its head stuck out of the barn's upper doors. Its horn. Its legs—we could hardly put our arms around them.

Aunt Oar raises her glass. The band can't hold against her booming voice. "Stop your dancing. I'm about to say somethin' now." It's easy to tell she has no idea what she will say, and her glass trembles.

"What color was the rhino?" Clara asks me. Lightly, lightly, she puts her fingers right there.

Rafters

At the bottom of Uncle D.A. and Aunt Cathy's steep driveway my mother asked me if I was lying. "No," I said, "I actually like them."

She turned up the air conditioner, listening for the right level of cold. She said, "We only want to treat family like family, for God's sake. If everybody else has given up on your uncle D.A. and aunt Cathy and their boys, all right. *We* are not ready. They'll change. Wait and see." I was twelve, so it was especially important to my parents to put me straight about patience. "Time Is The Teacher," they told me—a million times. They really believed everything always changed for the good or bad; in the early 1960s nothing and no one could escape change. I had to take their word for it that everything was plumb unless you knocked it out of plumb.

She said she couldn't stay, and asked me to say hello for her, and reminded me she'd be back after dinner, but I should call if I needed to. Before I was out of the car, Uncle D.A. tapped on her window. "Do I get him for the day?" he asked.

"If you act right," she said in a warning that was not even slightly playful. The only brother-and-sister resemblance was in their low hairlines and thick golden hair with fox-ear copperiness at the temples.

"Say hello to Cathy for me," my mother said, ready to back out of the driveway.

"She's makin' fudge," said Uncle D.A.

Her expression said, I'm warning you.

Aunt Cathy was in the bathroom where, according to Uncle D.A., people either were "makin' fudge" or "makin' tea" or "makin' fudge tea."

Uncle D.A. called to Aunt Cathy, "We got him for the day."

She would be pleased. She felt I was a good influence. I knew how to behave and to set an example; she always told me I was her favorite kid of all time and she hoped I wouldn't ever change.

Of course, Uncle D.A. and my cousins, A.D. and Bud, were a transforming influence on me. I had learned the infinite value of the nouns "fuckshit" and "motherfuck" (A.D. said it was uncool to say "motherfucker") and the verb "fuck" from them. Uncle D.A. could say "Fuck me" a hundred ways. "FuckME," confounded. "FUCKme," disgusted. "Fuck me," self-pitying.

In the kitchen, Bud asked, "How's it hangin'?" A.D. said, "Heytherezack."

"You're right on time," said Uncle D.A., pouring me coffee, black. My parents would never have thought of how horribly good a cup of coffee might taste to me.

I said thank you, which made him smile. Politeness of any kind made him smile derisively, so if I asked for another cup I'd command it: "Cuppa coffee." No one was allowed to be a fake in that house. You didn't pretend anything.

"Here's what comes first," said Uncle D.A., chewing something out from under his thumbnail. "We bring the pink stuff inside the house."

"Insulation," said Bud. "R22."

You learned that kind of thing there. What rating of insulation my parents' house had or how high the ceilings were or how far apart the wall studs were—I didn't know any of that. I was always the child in my own house, more a visitor there than I was at my uncle's house.

Uncle D.A. said, "A.D. and Zack here are a—"

"Ohfuck," said A.D.

"—team."

"What?" I said, "what?" because A.D.'s eyes were instantly full of spit.

Bud said, "It's fuckin' hot up there."

A.D. looked like he was going to cry. I called him a vadge. If I had said the word at home, I'd be slapped. I'd be slapped, I mean after my parents figured out it was short for vagina. Here, it was like saying "Amen" in church.

From the bathroom, Aunt Cathy said, "Jesus, Zack! Don't use that kind of language just becausa them." Who knew she was listening? She flushed and ran water in the sink and rummaged around loudly, but didn't leave the bathroom.

Uncle D.A. whispered, "She's doing her hair. For Zack."

"No shit," A.D. said.

Bud said, "No shit."

The toilet was still sucking and the pipes sonic-booming.

I've told all this before. And I've left things out. Now, before the part where Aunt Cathy hugs me like she's wiping my face against her breasts; before she tells me in front of Uncle D.A. and Bud and A.D. that I'm her one good apple, I'm going to jump ahead and tell how everything ended. I'm going to do it because the very end has to be included even if it isn't the part that matters.

So.

The end of it all came at about 4:30 in the morning. A.D. finally just missiled himself down through a hole in the kitchen ceiling. He sat up right after he landed, but he didn't say anything. He curled himself so his shoulders met his knees.

"You ARE fucked," said Bud. He said it with genuine pity, but he didn't go near. We didn't get in tight around A.D. or anything like that. We kept our distance. We had plenty of questions we could throw at that tiny trick match, eleven years old and burning no matter how hard you might blow at him.

"Jesus fuck me," said Uncle D.A.

"Goddamn," said Aunt Cathy, "it's a wonder you didn't break anything. Did you?"

"He looks okay," I lied.

In all the thirty-plus years since I was my parents' "good-faith effort" to reach out to their wayward relatives, I have gotten more like my Aunt Cathy and Uncle D.A. and less like my parents.

I love them. A.D. Bud. Aunt Cathy.

I love Uncle D.A. I do. Every couple summers, I drive from Las Almas, New Mexico, to Meltenville, Illinois, to get a dose of him.

He has multiple ailments; the pain, written all over him, makes him bigger than life.

Aunt Cathy. I see her sometimes, too. She has taken up archery since the divorce in '73. ("I'm Mr. Fuckme Custer if I get too close to her," Uncle D.A. says. "Thwip!" he says, thumping his fist to his heart.)

Bud and A.D. A.D. moves pianos, has his own crew paid by the hour, *A.D. Moving,* and they are very slow and very bad at it, according to A.D., and, according to him, they make a good living. Bud almost finished a Business major at the college. He builds coffins and coffin liners for O'Leary's Lasting Values Co. When I see the two of them, I steal them from their families (A.D. and Marlene have two teenage girls. Bud and Agnes have one, Rosy) who I bet have never once thought of me as a good apple. We go drinking at the U Dam Right bar where there are Vietnam vets who will buy Bud beer because he's one of them, and because in his college years he was the bartender. Bud tells them Johnson ruined my eye—my eye is another story—which starts conversations about how many people Kennedy, Johnson, and Nixon ruined, and Westmoreland and McNamara and Jesus. By the end of it, Bud and I have had a lot of free beer while A.D. has spent his kids' movie money trying to keep up. Bud and A.D. are always in work clothes because neither one has any other outfit, and I'm always in a suit because I don't either. People still dance like Elvis at U Dam Right. It's the Zero Millennium but nobody cares.

The End. That's it, the very end.

Okay.

The toilet was sucking. "Royal flush," said Uncle D.A. The pipes boomed. I haven't described him because I don't know how. This might help: sometimes he was swollen. His fingers and elbows and knees and his ankles, even his neck, would get puffy. A dozen years later I found out it was gout, and that you could take effective medicines for it, and that he wouldn't take the medicines.

To begin with, we pushed the living-room furniture to the walls, then started hauling in the big packages of unfaced pink fiberglass insulation.

Aunt Cathy ricocheted her way through the mess. When she saw me, she called, "Zack!" Real dramatic.

"Here he is!" A.D. said, dramatically. He shoved his fists in my back and pushed me forward to offer me up.

She shined my face against her breasts. She really did that. She was wearing a sleeveless sweatshirt and, underneath, no bra. She knew what she was doing and wasn't going to hold back. Or she didn't know what the hell she was doing and wasn't going to hold back. My mother would have screamed and snatched me away.

"You!" Aunt Cathy said to me. "He's got you working again, huh? My one good apple." With two fingers she scratched a star or something into my scalp. She wasn't my mom, or probably by then I would have made my body off limits to her the way you could tell A.D. and Bud had done. Twelve was that age for me when I wanted all my barbed-wire borders, I wanted people to cross into me and tear themselves to shreds crossing, but I couldn't have *told* you what I wanted from one damned minute to the next.

"Okay," I said, "o-KAY."

She didn't have tattoos. My parents said they were certain Aunt Cathy had tattoos, but I never saw any and I don't believe she kept secrets. She was what she was. She was small. I was eleven years old, and she wasn't much bigger than me.

It didn't take long for us to get the twenty-six packages of insulation in the house and then to take packages to the kitchen and to each of the two bedrooms. In Cathy and Uncle D.A.'s bedroom were the hi-fi and record collection. That was my first time in there, so I wanted to look at the records, but A.D. said, "Not *there*." I had it in my mind the records were Aunt Cathy's. "Can't I look?" I asked.

"His paycheck," said A.D. I already understood that the house was sawed in two. His paycheck. Her paycheck. Uncle D.A. and Aunt Cathy kept track of whose money bought what chair or set of tea glasses or record cabinet or records.

Before we left the bedroom A.D. nodded for me to look at something on the dresser. Rubbers. A half-dozen. In packages with a wincing Roman soldier on the front. Would my parents ever leave rubbers out where they could be seen? Ever?

"Are you boys taking an inventory?" Aunt Cathy said from the living room.

She made A.D. and me put on long pants, undershirts and long-sleeve khaki shirts that we had to button to our necks. "Fiberglass stings your skin," she said. I let her button my neck and sleeves. Because I couldn't stop her is why. "If you overheat," she said, "you quit right then, you hear?"

Bud and Uncle D.A. cut the bands off the packages in the living room. Bud was a natural laborer. At home, when my parents made me get out of the house to go play, or when they made me sign up for baseball or basketball, my dad would say, "Look at Bud and A.D.—they never get to play at all." Except for farms and sweatshops, parents don't work their kids nowadays, do they? Nobody approves. Bud and A.D. could work as long and as hard as grownups, and it seemed to me they felt good about it, all the work they had done on Uncle D.A.'s house and his garage full of industrial electrical outlet posts where he said he could teach me Electricity like he was teaching A.D. and Bud.

In fact, Bud and Uncle D.A. were in the mood for work now. They brought in brooms, dustpans, a stepladder.

Uncle D.A. set up the stepladder in a corner of the room, and popped out one narrow, long tile from the suspended ceiling. When the tile crumbled pretty badly along the edges, he said, "Fuckme!" with weird joy. He had been raised like a worker. ("You can be raised like a dickhead worker or raised like a pussy," he always said. "Which way you want?")

He dropped the tile to the floor. When he came down the ladder he stood on the tile like it was his little stage. He snarled, "Listen up!" at Aunt Cathy. He held the screwdriver upside down, put his lips right on the handle, and sang, "Numbah fawty-seven say to numbah three, 'You da cutest jailbird I evah did see.'" Aunt Cathy batted her eyelashes at Uncle Elvis.

I was sing-thinking the next words, *I sure would be delighted with your company*. There was a rhythm there. I could fit into it. I wanted to be part of it.

A.D. was already climbing up the ladder. "Come on," he said.

I put my gloves on, brand-new leather gloves from Aunt Cathy, and followed him up.

Hold it. There's a part I left out of the beginning.

Well, actually, I left out a lot.

This won't take too long.

Once, one day, my family and their family did get together. We all went to the two-block zoo in Alton. Even when I was twelve the Alton Zoo seemed like what it was: two blocks long. This was a few months after Uncle D.A. had volunteered to prune my parents' peach tree. With his bare hands, he had stripped off branches—big ones and small ones, he called them all "suckers"—and even after my mother begged him to stop, he ripped and twisted and cracked off limbs, saying, "It's a sucker, Rita. I know what I'm doin'."

Time is the teacher. The tree thrived after that.

When Time inclined my mother to forgive and forget, we went to the zoo where we all got along fine but where (I'm only guessing now) my parents decided to never ever invite them to our home even though I would be sent to their home once in a while as a "good-faith effort."

What happened is that A.D. dared me to mash my face on the glass of the herpetological exhibit, which I wouldn't do, which led him to call me a vadge, which caused no problem since my parents didn't hear any of it.

A.D. kept at it. He got Bud to join in.

I brought up swimming snakes. "Do you think you could out-swim a venomous snake?" I asked.

Bud said no, of course not.

"Could you, A.D.?"

"Maybe," he said. "They swim faster than the ones with no poison?"

"We can't swim," said Bud. "Neither one of us."

I knew that already. And I knew they'd never been in a boat

when I asked if they ever water-skied. I said my mother's words before I thought twice about who would hear them: "Being in a boat
is the free-est feeling."

"You vadge," Bud said. "Who the fuck wants to be in a frying pan
on the water?"

A.D. tapped the glass cage over the four or five lazy "Snakes of
the Desert Southwest." They stretched unwildly around volcanic
rocks painted phosphorescent white.

"I'll teach you to swim sometime if you want," I said to A.D.

"Yeah," he said. "That would be the free-est feeling."

At the aviary Bud wanted me to answer him about whether,
when, where, and exactly how I masturbated. *"Teach us,"* he said.
We had a shouting match loud enough to upset some of the birds. It
ended about the time our parents caught up with us.

None of that caused the problem.

Later in the day, A.D. showed me how to bend over and crunch
my thumb against one side of my nose so I could blow a thick, unbroken noodle of booger out of the other side. He'd wipe some of
the mucus on your neck if you didn't duck quick.

I learned well. A week after the zoo expedition I did it expertly
when I thought my parents weren't looking. I had to explain who
taught me.

Actually, they already knew.

Now, I'll tell all the rest.

I put my hands on the rungs of the ladder to follow A.D. like the
astronaut Wally Schirra climbing the steps into the Mercury-Atlas.
These days they come in all sizes, but in those days astronauts
were never allowed to be over five feet tall. You had to have guts
but you had to be a shrimp. I could see that A.D. and I had been
chosen for the rafter crew because we had half the qualifications of
Wally Schirra. I pushed my shoulders toward my ears to squeeze
into the rafters.

"In 'er?" asked Uncle D.A.

I spider-crawled over the web of ceiling joists. My eyes were still adjusting when A.D. spit "Boo!" into the back of my head. I lost the butt-and-hands part of my balance but somehow stayed on with my sprawled legs or I would have fallen right through. "Fuck you!" I shouted. That and "Boo!" reverberated so much my head clanged like a bell.

"Lez rock!" That was Uncle D.A.'s Elvis voice.

"Honey," Aunt Cathy asked, "watch it now."

"Evahbody, lez rock!"

Bud said, "Ready?" up at us.

With one word A.D. asked a long question. "Bud?"

Nobody answered him.

For about an hour they pushed the nine-and-a-half-foot strips of insulation up into the hole in the ceiling. A.D. left it to me to grab and pull through. He dragged the strips somewhere in the darkness and grunted them into place.

"Fit it," said Uncle D.A. "Don't fuck it up." He poked the ceiling near the ladder. "Push it down—you listenin'?—make it fit." I thought he was joking with us.

"We ain't stupid," said A.D.

More insulation, a piece torn a little, squirmed through the hole. I grabbed, pulled. All the faint light up there came from beneath us; it reached through the ceiling tiles, which were made of silica and what Uncle D.A. called "mineral wood." I mention it because he made things up if he didn't know. I learned a lot from him, but I haven't figured out what parts to trust.

A.D. scrambled out of the darkness to take the strip from me. As if our eyes had just at that moment adjusted to the darkness, we stared at each other.

I ground the insulation right into his sweaty face. I didn't have a reason in the world to be mean to him. But in Uncle D.A.'s house I had permission to do things without any reasons.

"Fucker!" he said.

Uncle D.A. poked another place on the ceiling where he was guessing A.D. would be. "Fit it!"

A.D. rubbed his eyes with his shirtsleeves. "You're making it worse," I said. I'd got him right in the eyes, and it felt good. I was a kid. I didn't know about how dangerous fiberglass was. But I knew that A.D. was going to get me back the first chance he got.

For the next couple of hours he kept rubbing while he worked, and his eyes started weeping. Making things worse was something A.D. knew how to do perfectly.

"Where are you?" Uncle D.A. said, poking the tiles to show us where we were supposed to be.

"Right here," I said, whether we were on his target or not. He couldn't tell.

"You fuckin' with me?" he said once. I didn't answer. A.D. didn't answer. As a matter of fact, A.D. had stopped talking by then. We were slick with sweat and our skin glowed red and we scratched ourselves like heated-up grasshoppers. Sometimes when I pushed the insulation his way, A.D. acted like maybe he couldn't see it.

From another room, the room next to the room we were above, Aunt Cathy said she wanted us to come down for lunch. Uncle D.A. said it wasn't even eleven. He banged with whatever it was he was banging. The rafters were so close over me and the tiles so close under me, my skin felt like the skin of a drum. When he shouted, "Make it fit!" and "Where are you?" I was surprised at how much words could hurt, like being slapped hard.

We finished with the living room by laying the last strip over the hole where the tile had been removed four hours earlier. "No more," I said.

"Break time!" said Aunt Cathy.

Uncle D.A. shouted, "Kitchen next!" When he poked the kitchen ceiling, I scrambled there like a trained monkey. A.D. stayed put. To be sure he had heard, I said, "Break time."

"I heard."

Beneath us, Aunt Cathy said something to Uncle D.A. and Bud. My guess was that she was insisting Uncle D.A. let us all eat. Bud asked something, asked it again, and got answered, "You pussy!"

The next thing I heard was the living-room ceiling tile pulled back into place. We were sealed off from all of it down there.

Across from me, A.D. gave me some kind of grasshopper twitch or astronaut salute, which made me want to sit next to him. But if

I did that for him I was a vadge and if I did it for me I was a homo, that much we both knew.

About fifteen minutes later, the tile was popped off in the kitchen. Bud popped it, but disappeared. We heard what was going on. They were eating.

Aunt Cathy said, "Zack, we're—"

"Fuckin' right!" Uncle D.A. stamped a foot or hit a table. "We're eating! We're hungry! It's hot down here, you know it?"

Bud said, "We'll bring some up."

Uncle D.A. said, "Soon as we finish putting the kitchen insulation in."

I asked if they would send up some water. Just that fast, I knew I should have demanded the water because Bud and Aunt Cathy were listening for how Uncle D.A. listened.

"Give us some fuckin' water," I said.

Aunt Cathy said, "Don't you talk that way!"

A.D. either gulped or giggled. Or both—I couldn't tell. His eyes were like busted play-gun caps. The swollen skin under his sharp, short lashes glistened.

We scrambled to the center of the crawl space where we could lean back against the big ridge beam. I said, "The kitchen's small. We'll finish quick. Won't we?"

A.D. stared down at the ceiling joists, and his head nodded, maybe counting how many strips of insulation we would put in between the joists before it was all over. He shoved the heels of his hands into his eyes. Hurting himself worse.

"Stop that shit!" I said. They had to have heard me down there, and they must have wondered. They went on eating. Aunt Cathy, and Bud, too.

A.D. was Albert David. Bud, who was thirteen, was really named Rosario. Rosario was the name of Aunt Cathy's once-upon-a-time teenage husband. Since the evolution of Bud's name made me curious, maybe it does others: kids called him Rose or Rosy until he beat them up; they called him Rosebud if they wanted to get beat up again. When the fights were over, they called him Bud.

The usual story of a stupid name. It's mean of me to tell it. (His middle name was Angel.) But I put it in because it explains why Bud and A.D. never called me "Floater" the way other kids did. I had a lazy left eye. Bud had the name. A.D. had Bud as a brother. The usual story. I shouldn't have put it in.

A.D.'s head counted, nodded and counted something or a lot of somethings. Pretty soon, my head counted and nodded. The rafters and joists looked to me like the whole skull of the house. I guess any building depends as much on its rafters as on its foundation. Emptiness has to be in balance with solidness, right?

The roof was like a nose cone where the air and the light behaved wrong. We sat awhile, which only made me dizzy. We were in the skull and orbiting, it felt like. We were in the air, and stirred up and weightless and nowhere near solid ground.

Why did I shove the insulation in A.D.'s face? "I shouldn't've," I said. "I shouldn't've fucked up your eyes."

"No shit," he said. He scratched the back of his head against the ridge beam, and the beam conducted his misery to my own head. And to my left eye.

We nodded and counted and scratched our heads and backs and wet necks. I tried to toughen up, not to be a vadge, not in front of A.D. "Fuckme," I said, trusting I could hold everything back by saying that the right way. "FuckME."

"Fuck you very much," he said.

I blurted out, "I apologize, A.D. Honest. I'm sorry."

He knocked his head against mine. Hard. It hurt so much it made me sob. I apologized again.

He got quiet. He was accepting my apology, I could tell. He said, "Grow up, Zack."

I was thankful to him for helping get it all over with. We shrugged it off.

After they sent up the next strip of insulation, Bud poked his head in. He whispered, "Zack, A.D. Come down and eat." He dropped back down so fast you couldn't be sure he had been there.

"Did you hear?" I asked. A.D. ignored me.

Uncle D.A. banged the tiles on the opposite side from us. "Start here!" he yelled. He told Aunt Cathy to stop something-or-other, and then he said, "And stop moaning like a jackass." I heard part of what she was saying, which I think she must have been saying to Bud: "I don't know if we should."

The ceiling jumped. "Start here!"

A.D. put down the insulation he had hold of. He rubbed his eyes. Godzilla always rubbed his eyes in the Godzilla movies. Does anybody remember that? He scrambled to the place Uncle D.A. banged. With a blind jump, he crashed his legs through the tiles and caught the joists with his hands so he would not fall all the way to the floor below. You can imagine what that did to his hands. He said, "Hello. Anybody home?"

"FuckME!" Uncle D.A. beat A.D.'s legs and ankles. I figured what he was thwacking A.D. with was a broomstick.

"A.D.!" Aunt Cathy shouted.

"He's okay," said Bud, and he asked, "A.D., you okay?"

Uncle D.A. screamed, "Fuckshit! A.D.! A.D.?" He called up to me: "Zack?"

"He's okay," I said. A.D. was already scrambling over to another joist and making himself into a skewer. This time, he only crashed through as far as his knees. He caught the joists, and swim-kicked his legs, and pulled up, and looked down through the hole where the broom handle whipped at him.

Uncle D.A. stung the walls, the floor; his breathing started to sound like buzzing.

"All right!" said Uncle D.A., as final as a human voice can get. He banged the broom handle once, real hard, on one tile. A.D. scrambled to that particular tile and hammered his legs through to his knees and screwed himself around to break out as much of the tile as possible, I guess. I think Uncle D.A. tried to grab his legs but missed.

"I'm coming down," I said, and right at the same time Uncle D.A. said, "Get your asses down here."

A.D. caught up with me. "Please," he said. He shoved his shirt-sleeves up at my face, and I said, "Huh?" but I unbuttoned them for him. Then, when I could look closer and see that his hands were bloody and swollen and that his left one had what looked like a broken thumb and maybe broken fingers, I unbuttoned the collar and the front buttons for him. I helped him take the shirt off.

He backed up from me.

"What do you want?" I asked. "You want to go down there? What are you waiting for?" He didn't know what he wanted.

I turned him around enough to get my hands on his back. Up near his neck where I gripped him, he was muscular, the sheaths of strength there felt invulnerable. What I did is something I just knew to do. What I did is I scratched his back. His shoulder blades, and along his spine. And under his arms and on his sides. He turned himself this way and that to make it easier. It took what seemed like a long time because of all the silence between us.

Downstairs everyone was also quiet, and between A.D. and me, well, the silence was finally too much. Too much, so I stopped. I thought what would come next was him calling me a vadge.

He moved his jaw, chewing up and swallowing almost all of what he was going to say. He said, "Zack. Stay in touch."

"Sure," I said. What was I supposed to say? I felt ready to run away from him and from me, whoever it was I'd just been; and I did, I charged down the ladder. I expected Uncle D.A. to charge up it.

He didn't. The only way my uncle could have ever gotten into A.D.'s narrow crawl space was to become a whole lot smaller than he was.

He looked up the ladder, looked far up it, probably amazed that it went so much farther than any of us thought. He shrugged. He beat the shit out of the ladder with the broom handle, then wrestled it to the ground where he kicked in its cheap aluminum rungs by jumping on them. He had bought it with his paycheck and it was his to destroy if he wanted.

When we heard tiles bust in the master bedroom, we followed Uncle D.A. there. We waited. The feet and legs punched through another tile, flailed around, disappeared. Tile fragments and dirt rained down on the bed. And on the rubbers.

Aunt Cathy said, "We don't have the money to fix it with." She didn't seem to be talking to any of us.

The Wrecker punched out three more tiles. We could hear him doing some kind of flamenco on the boards, panting.

Bud said, "You ain't gettin' lunch now, motherfuck." His voice was calm, admiring. For a long time after he said it, nothing happened.

We went to work. We threw the rubble into the middle of the rooms, and didn't bother with trash cans. We all worked in different rooms. I noticed how we were all apart like that. I noticed because when my family cleaned house we worked together in one room at a time and we talked and horsed around and forgot who was doing what, which was stupid and inefficient and meant we never really did a good job.

Bud said, "He's done."

A.D. didn't come down. I offered to go up after him but Aunt Cathy said, "Let him be, now."

Uncle D.A., who was in one of the bedrooms, said to Aunt Cathy, "You know what he's doin'?"

"What?" she said, but now Uncle D.A. put his head back and spoke up at the ceiling: "What are you doin'?"

From the back bathroom, Bud asked, "Should I go up?"

"No," I said, "don't go up there."

"A.D.," Uncle D.A. said, "answer me. What are you doin'?"

It made sense to me he wouldn't answer.

"Like a damned child," Uncle D.A. said.

In the kitchen again, he punched through. We went there and watched the ceiling grow legs three more times.

In the evening, my mother showed up. Aunt Cathy and Uncle D.A. invited her inside. Aunt Cathy said, "Don't get all upset now, Rita."

Picture that house. It'd make most people find Jesus. Or lose him. My mother wanted me home "this very minute" and said she deserved an explanation. I demanded to be allowed to stay overnight. Before she could tell me, "Certainly not," Uncle D.A. said, "We gotta fuckin' crisis here. We need him."

"We need him for the night," said Aunt Cathy, squeezing my arm in her two dirty hands. We were all standing near the open front door, but gazing inside not outside.

My mother looked Aunt Cathy over as if she were trying to discover the hidden tattoos. "He's—this isn't good for Zack," she said.

Uncle D.A. said, "The hell it's not!"

I told her A.D. was my best friend in the world. "This is all my fault," I said. I said leaving him wouldn't be fair. "He wouldn't leave me if it was me!"

She wasn't convinced. She stared straight at Uncle D.A.

"Fuuu-uuck meee, fuuck-uuck-MEE," said Uncle D.A. like someone singing "Amazing Grace" in the electric chair. She still wasn't convinced.

Right then, a voice came from heaven. Actually.

"Please," A.D. said. His mouth must have been right up against one of the tiles. "Let Zack stay."

It scared my mother into wrapping her arms around herself, backing up to the door frame, and leaning on it. "We *are* going," she said.

I shook off Aunt Cathy's hands. One word at a time, I commanded my mother: "Stay here with us. Or get out."

"You will not—"

"Get out!"

Aunt Cathy said, "Zack!"

"You will not talk to me like that!" said my mother.

"Just did," Bud said.

"Get out!"

"I'll bring your father!"

"Bring him," Bud said, the executioner's assistant.

My mother said, "I will."

Uncle D.A. turned her on her heels toward the door. "We need him," he said.

"I'm sending your father!" she shouted at me. "You get in that car right now!"

Uncle D.A. hustled her to the car. He promised, "Things're going to change for the good around here. Give us time."

"It's too late—for all of you!" my mother said.

We were already back in the house as she drove away.

"What'll she do? Ground you?" Bud said. I felt like I was part of his finest moment. When I swallowed that down, it burned, then it felt good, then sickening.

"I'm in the living room," A.D. announced. His voice didn't travel down naturally. It poured through all the holes all at once.

A tapping sound came from the living-room ceiling. A.D. was testing a tile by tapping it with his feet or he was tapping his hands or his head against something. A decision-making-type sound. He would be up there forever, or down right away. Taptap, taptaptaptap.

Before the sound stopped, a part of a tile turned yellow. Then yellower. A surprising amount of piss, probably his whole load.

He crashed tiles all night.

We cleaned up after him, not talking to him or to each other, only quietly waiting like anybody would during a bombing. The junk hit the velour recliner that came out of Uncle D.A.'s paycheck; it narrowly missed the matching Buddha lamps but didn't spare the giant dried flowers that came out of Aunt Cathy's paycheck. Anything that represented their hard work, hers and Uncle D.A.'s and Bud's and A.D.'s work, was a target.

Turning off the lamps, Bud said, "Your dad ain't coming tonight."

"He'll come in the morning," I said. My parents worked on the same road-construction crew, different shifts. They didn't have as much as Aunt Cathy and Uncle D.A., but they were proud they lived another lifestyle.

Bud pointed a finger at me and said in an adult voice, "Have you learned your lesson, young man?" I sure can't begin to tell how sorry I felt for him.

Jumping onto the insulation, A.D. kicked down twenty or thirty big pink blisters, until he knocked out almost the whole living-room ceiling. At about four in the morning, he stopped, again.

Aunt Cathy dusted herself off. She said to the ceiling, "I'm going to the potty. I can't hold it anymore."

In the bathroom she whimpered and wailed and talked to herself. Eventually, she started talking to me. "Zack. They won't let you come here no more, will they?"

Uncle D.A. said, "Your parents are assholes, Zack. We're assholes, too, that's fuckin' obvious. But we don't pretend."

Aunt Cathy rummaged around but didn't leave the bathroom. "Do you think we been wrong? A.D.'s just a kid."

I said, "He is not."

She trickled water in the bathroom sink, which made the pipes squeal. She turned the water off and splashed around loudly.

"Get out of the shitter!" said Uncle D.A.

Bud said, "Yeah," but he barely said it.

When she talked again, she sounded like she was talking through a towel. "Aren't you ashamed of us, Zack? Isn't everybody going to be ashamed of us?"

"Yes," I said simply, without thinking.

That made Uncle D.A. stir. He said, "Get off your ass and sweep." He nudged Bud, who didn't move from the rocker he was rocking in. He nudged me.

"Fuck you," I said.

He didn't like it. He grabbed up the wrecked ladder in the kitchen and banged it into the ceiling. "I'm coming up, you sorry little fuck. You're going to be a sorrier little fuck."

Uncle D.A. wasn't going anywhere. He shook the ladder the way a prisoner shakes the bars in prison movies.

Directly overhead, A.D. was crouched and looking down. He looked down at all of us but saw nothing. The next time the ladder was rattled up at him, he unleashed a big God's laugh.

We laughed with him. Bud first. Aunt Cathy. Uncle D.A. Me.

The people who own pianos

for Rick

We never can find their fuckin' houses.

We get a set of shit directions there, a different set of shit directions back. Okay, we've got an attitude about the goddamn load no matter what we're told it is—grand, baby, stand-up, damaged, used, good used, or good—fifth or first floor, basement, attic, narrow or wide staircase—the kit or the whole coffin—it's the same to *A.D. Moving.*

We carry it out into the light beyond the lighted, decorated, dimwit room we rearrange, rip, gouge, and nick all we want on our way out. Make way, we say, make way—words that give us rights greater any day than the owners', am I right?

Some are widows, widowers, divorcees or divorcers, retiring or retired. They are not as sensitive as you would think. We're hauling off something they wanted bad or still want, but they won't complain, it's like they can't. They stall out, clamp up, they stutter those fucked witty things we never get or ever got.

What makes us us and them not us? What makes them them and us not them? They were politely chewing when we were swallowing hard. That's how they were, that's how they are. They learned putting together when we were learning pulling apart.

So fucking what? So, fucking what? So-fucking-what.

We amputate the legs, mummify the sound and the keyboards in blankets, rope and tape, and cart the thing to freedom, taking no educated guesses ever about how the damned load has gotten in there, how the fuck it will get out, how many hours we'll take making way and making way and making way. You do this job long

143

enough you can't think of anything good to say about the people who own pianos, with their walk-in closets and their screened-in porches, their Eurostyle custom kitchens, wet bars, hot tubs, and blond Mexican tiles.

Everything we scar scars that bandaged monster we bump against the plaster or wallpaper. We make the walls drum, the floors groan. We strike the chandeliers and bronze standing lamps, strum the dumb leggy houseplants these people hang in jute from their ceilings.

Fuck yeah, they're the people who macramé and refurbish and antique—or would, or have that look like they might. They might, they might, they might, they say, and never have to speak it, do they? Whatever they want they only have to say they want it once.

I love them.

I love the people who own pianos decorated with some shredded piece of lace or crochet they want to tell you the story of. I hate their stories about some other piano in some foreign country someone fled for some reason that has to be recited, for some reason, and can't just be said. I hate their sad, ugly mugs, but I love them, and I tell them, Hey, A.D. loves you, you buttfucks, that's why I'm here—to ease your pain at Your Time of Loss. See, I brought my best crew of compassionate men. They love you, too. They do. Right, guys? Hourly employees. Hourly they love you.

(Okay, all right, I don't say any of that to the people who own pianos. You can't say that shit to them.)

If they want, they can talk. God, they can talk. They can. You can listen. One time, this guy says to the crew—and the crew was all parked on his couch because he told us to—he made us—he was about to fuckin' cry—he called us "Boys,"—he said, "Boys, our dog has gone to prison, boys. For life."

A strange thing to hear from an old guy sitting alone at his worthless stand-up piano with no "our" in sight, one chair at his table, one empty glass at his place, who probably meant "our son," "our grandson," or "our minister" has gone to prison, but couldn't have meant the dog unless it was another dog than the haunted-looking, balding red hound dog cowering like a convict or ex-con against the piano pedals and gumming a rubber doll baby that kept its eyes and mouth shut, its arms and legs straight out.

"Boys," the old man said, "*I* was a piano mover," gray boogers floating in both his eyes. "Can you believe it?"

Fuck no, we thought. Fuck no, I said. Oh, hell no, I didn't really say it, I couldn't, but I must've almost-did because he made a snorting sound and said, "Fuck, yes."

The people who own pianos are never people who moved them. He couldn't've been the player. It couldn't've been his piano.

"Get off my bed," he growled. His bed? Hell. It might've been a foldout or something, how do you know, because their couches aren't always couches, and their groomed, good-looking dogs are more like blue or yellow budgies in sparkling wire cages. He couldn't've been the owner. It couldn't've been his dog.

"Our dog was the one who played," he said. Probably meant "our daughter," "our granddaughter," "our ghost," "our god" played this monster. We got up anyway. We petted his dog, named after that prick Judge Bork. It was on his tags. "Hey, get this," we said to the old guy who couldn't have got, owned it, named it. "Bork," we said. "Bork!" Bork never moved, never stretched, yawned, scratched, twitched. Just chewed on the doll's eight toes, and hummed and made the old man's same snoring sound. "Fetch," we said, and threw the old man's magazines and sheet music and sofa pillows and shit like that at Bork's head, with no results.

But the old man. The old man on his piano bench, flinched, bent, and all of a sudden he thumped the closed key cover, and said, like it meant something, "Piss on it." He meant on it all, the whole thing, piano, piano makers, buyers, sellers, players, movers, traders, and the entire damn unjust prison system, but at first we thought he wanted us to lift our legs and piss on his dog, and we looked at Bork like he was a fire hydrant, and he might've been he might've been, he was that red and that immovable and stupid.

He said, "Piss on it" again, which we didn't. He said, "Do you know who I am?" which we didn't. He said, "Of course not," and shook his head.

I guess that's when we decided to screw him over. Love is like that, you know.

We took the piano, took the couch, the table; took the one chair, the one glass, the magazines and sheet music. We took the rubber doll baby. The last thing we did was shovel Bork onto the piano cart and roll him out like the royal dog he was or the genie or dragon or troll who played the old man's piano really well before he did a life sentence and died and came back as a red dog. Make way, make way, we said. And the old man did.

Hell, we are different, to be honest. So-fucking-what. So fucking what? They never cuss. We cuss. They tell the truths that lie; we tell the lies that lie, and that's the truth. The people who own pianos never share the stories they are most ashamed to share, and that's no lie. That's how they are, that's how they were.

We are different, us and them, them and us. They were learning rest when we were learning restless. Oh, fuck yeah, sometimes we have to put the damned thing on the floor or the stairs. Or we get as far as the front yard, and lay it down there that loving way you lay down a tire you just busted off a rim. We rest our backs or heads on the hard pillow, the hard lost island of overambitious under-talented piano bangers, the hard silent coffin you could fit three little Mozarts and their wigs inside. We slap the black giant on its ass or pet its smooth, hard chest, or we make a guess at middle C and play muffled "Chopsticks" through the ropes and tape and blankets. What? Did you think we never knew people who knew the people who played pianos?

Well, we did.

And all the people who own pianos stare at us through their clean front windows or lean out their solid walnut doors or stand on but not beyond the front edges of their long driveways and lawns. They don't like our cussing, laughing, or our doll we call "Sleeping Ugly" asleep on the dash, dreaming of an open mouth and open eyes; dreaming of two more toes, of chewing on the dog to show him what it's like; dreaming of some clothes, for God's sake, to cover her genitals, and some cash to cover her ass on the short fall into trouble and the long climb out of it; dreaming of a

halfway house or a hospital room or a cardboard box on a steel
steam grate; dreaming of toothaches and nosebleeds and rubber
or—why not?—real scabs, and nails to pick the scabs; and dreaming of prescription drugs and sex toys and sleeplessness—fabulous
fucking sleeplessness. And teeth. And a tongue—and the spit to go
with it. And bile. And blockage and gas and life-size shit, and no
bitchy sisters and no goddamn prince. Dreaming of leaving home
with a mean red dog and criminal friends in a dangerous ride on the
black vinyl prow of a speeding van.

(Okay, okay, she's not dreaming of any of that. Probably not. Probably not. So-fucking-what. So, fucking what? Soooooo fuuuuuuck-
ing what?)

They don't like us.

They don't like our dog's erotic dancing, and they hate the ap-
plause when we applaud ourselves. They don't like our need to
know the kind of happiness they knew before they needed something else.

Last Will

Sons should play with their fathers. Why should they ever stop?

Here is your chance to fit my left shoe on my right foot, my right on the left.

Poise a booger—mine or your own is fine—onto the stiff tip of my index finger.

Spill soup over my chin, my shirtfront, and, deeper than I would, dip my elbows in the bowl. You can make me smell like a pot of chili and American cheese if you want. And if you don't—hell then, don't.

I won't rest any worse when you prop me up and lever open my mouth to push cornbread or beans in under my nose. Forget the tablecloth, forget the napkins.

Spit a gobber on me, on my pants crotch, my bald spot, on my tie knot.

Sons should play with their fathers! Why should they ever stop?

The conveyor belt at the airport. The dressing room at the mall. The rail of a movie balcony. I can turn and change and fall at your will. I will. I can be lifted, dropped, rolled, pulled, folded, packed.

I can be driven to a bar, my blue fists tied to a mechanical bullride. Two-bit cigar. Magic-Marker mustache. Ten-gallon hat. Fringed chaps. You can position me in a paddleboat, high chair, on a donut rack, diving board. Electrified prison fence.

Given the chance to do it, what son would not? At a time like this I represent a whole new group of choices. What other options have you got for me except the ash pot, the dark pit?

If I had been allowed, I would have set my own dead dad, restless in the afterlife, atop the family tree, the very point of the forty-foot cypress uncentered on the plot of our front yard.

I tell you—no matter what your grandmother said—your grandfather would have wanted to be posthumously hazardous. He wouldn't have minded one bit that mean tribute.

Sons should play with their fathers! Why should they ever stop? I would take him back up the cypress when he fell, and, no matter who or what he crushed, I would pay the fine to the police and not explain and not apologize for him, though I might say the obvious: He is my dad. I look up to him. He tumbles from great heights—and is pointless. He does some damage—and is damaged. He cannot be replaced nor rehabilitated, not by anyone. Not by his sons.

Then I would shoulder him up the ladder and lift him back, the one man I most loved, onto his tiny, tiny cypress throne, king of the wind, my dethroned king, the one man I most hated in the few minutes I ever hated him. I would deliver him again and again, like a reused Easter basket; I'd take him to the flame tip of that regal evergreen, that version of salvation he would have most appreciated.

In death I want to be the cause of some small rough justice—not for me—not for me—I've been crowned in curses and blessed enough.

What I wish, dear sons, is that you play with me, that I show you myself tender, that you give me yourselves rough, that you laugh at my empty grave until you lose your breath—but only one—one breath.

THE COMPLETE HISTORY OF NEW MEXICO

PART III:
THE CANNED FOOD TIME IN NEW MEXICO

Mr. Belter:

Your footnotes and bibliographic references to Sir Arthur Conan Doyle do not support your claims. Your footnotes and bibliography are incorrect in format. I instructed you to cite artwork as "Courtesy of," not "Owned by." Have you lost your guidelines? Your stepmother's punctuation and usage have improved. You and your stepmother must review comma usage and rules of coherence if she continues, improperly, to be your editor.
    MINUS 8 points.

Your illustrations appear to be photographs of painted floor tiles. I must see the original artwork at once, and, without further delay, you must provide me with information proving the existence of Mr. Rush Bradbridger.
    MINUS 5 points.

All of your supporting evidence is questionable. The false testament you have given regarding your friends is reprehensible. Your libelous misquoting of your teacher's remarks is a very serious matter that can only be corrected if you agree to destroy the entire essay at once. Your stepmother will, I know, agree with me on this matter.
    MINUS 3 points.

I do not dispute that you own a good reversible jacket. I do not dispute its special personal value. Why must you insist that the jacket is a gift from me? As a matter of principle I do not offer gifts to my students, ever. I do not murder for them. I do not smuggle them across borders. I don't love them. I don't love them. I don't love them.

84 of 100 points = B

Mrs. D. Bettersen

The Canned Food Time In New Mexico

by Charlemagne J. Belter
Sixth Grade
Mrs. Dorothy Betterson
November 25 1966

MY OUTLINE

The Introduction
    A) God Glasses
    B) Armorers
        1) spidermallows
        2) faith room
    C) Canning
    D) Side Effects
        1) The Human System
        2) monks and mescal and labels
        3) Dominicans founded
    E) Poison Spoons

I.   Photography
    A) Conan Doyle
    B) The Silent Places
        1) cucharas
    C) Mrs. B's Reversible Gift
    D) Sun
    E) Daguerreotype
    F) The Spirit Album
    G) The Mesmeric Disembodiment of Spirits
    H) Emulsion

II. Society
    A) Kodak
    B) Slave Descendants
    C) Unreliable Sources
    D) Spoon Illness
        1) Mr. Bret Harte's chemicals and ruby lamps
        2) writing books

III. Higher Places
    A) Ex-votos
        1) hammered cans
        2) candle negatives
        3) miracles
        4) religious realisms
    B) Mrs. B's Real Name
    C) Love in the Mesilla Valley
        1) Mr. Alvarezo
        2) students
        3) Daniel's dad
        4) Marty and Daniel
        5) Marty and the Mesilla Valley

IV. The Story Complete
    A) The Miracle of the Fire Goats
    B) Faith and History and Hiding
    C) The Jacket
    D) The Miracle of the Red Felt Hat
    E) Falling and Falling Asleep
    F) The Mexico Expedition
        1) chess
        2) the lifeboat industry
    G) Mounds and Women
    H) The Miracle of the Guitarron
    I) Proof

THE CANNED FOOD TIMES IN NEW MEXICO

My Introduction

When there was first canned food in New Mexico was when people found God again. A lot of people were looking before that but it's like when my stepmother loses her glasses and needs them to find her glasses.

And so they were Godless until they found God which was when they found canned food and also photography. The Canned Food Time in what wasn't even called New Mexico yet was about the time when armor was going out of style[1] and what were you going to do if you were an armorer? You canned.

You canned refried beans. Pig parts and snake meat and chorizo and spidermallows. They roasted big white spiders they called malos and the female ones malas and could have made smores or smoras because they already had crackers and chocolate bars in those times. It's not something I know—it's something I believe— and that's why it can't go in here. There is no room for Faith in History is what Mrs. Bettersen says who might not think I hear her sometimes. I hear her real good.

This was about 1898. I got into sixth grade but almost not. Iron could be made into a thin plate and you could coat that plate with tin and you could can all you wanted if you had a canning machine that can make a flat thing curved and a curved thing closed. People from everywhere wanted some armored food. They didn't mind side effects because side effects come every time you invent the electric guitar or hair curlers or the kickstand and so people didn't complain. There was leeching into The Human System of canned food poison.[2]

There was illuminated labels that monks made and gum made from mescal plants to put the labels on and the monks chewed on it and had visions and you should see some of those labels they made. The monks had canning machines that make an open thing closed and a closed thing sealed. The most famous monk guy was

Friar Dominic who founded the Dominicans in The Canned Food Times.[3]

There was the invention of little spoons called cucharas so you could eat right from the can. And it turns out the spoons were poison. The poisoned people felt all the time like they had to sing and talk and tell whatever happened to them. It got loud wherever there was canned goods and wherever there was canned goods people heard and saw God and wanted more. Nobody had any radios yet no stereos or like that but this is about when the Indians and the Spanish of the Mesilla Valley started wanting them. And people were always looking at themselves on the backs or in the little faces of the polished spoons and then eating and eating and singing and talking. And praying. They have some of the spoons in the Hatch Museum and if you don't ask Mr. Stephen Burhart there he won't bring them out because he says he has his reasons.

Photography

One thing that happened was photography and the visit of Conan
Doyle and I'll get to that but the worse thing was that the poisoned
people which was everyone including children and the last of the
teenage slaves forgot to feed the horses and dogs and goats. Lots of
the animals couldn't stand starving and all the noise and they ran
away into The Silent Places around Deming and Lordsburg[4] where
they untamed themselves and mated way too much. And now you've
got a whole worldwide Spam industry because of them.

You talk about side effects. When Mrs. Bettersen who is you—
you're the only one reading my essay except for my stepmother
who types it and says she thinks it's all good but she's happy she's
not my teacher. When Mrs. Bettersen gives me my bad grades she
always says "You reap what I sow."

I took her which is you to where the rose mounds once were.
She said I sounded like a liar even if I said I'm not.

I offered to show Mrs. Bettersen the cucharas in the Hatch
Museum and we phoned Mr. Burhart from my school but we got
Mrs. Midge Burhart and she said What spoons? She told me later
there were spoons all right and she showed me them. They were
small because people's mouths were small then. On the backs of
the spoons I could see my face coming out to see me and on the
fronts I could see my face in the little faces of them going far away
and afraid.

When Mrs. Bettersen hung up the school phone at the Counselor's
Office which was empty she said she had a gift for me. She wanted
me to have a gift she was going to give me if I would let her tell
me the truth and if I would write it down and turn it in to the one
person which is Mrs. Bettersen which is you who will know it is
true but who is going to say it isn't if my stepmother or anybody
else ever asks.

She drove us toward Hatch but not like we were going there.

The gift from Mrs. Bettersen is a reversible man's jacket and I
have it to keep but my stepmother says it doesn't prove anything

and she says that only makes her sad. On one side it is dark brown leather with red ribbing and on the other side red cotton with dark brown leather ribbing. The red part is soft. It feels good.

Sometimes I would see my friend Daniel wearing the reversible jacket and sometimes his sister Marty wore it and I had to ask Mrs. Bettersen about that. But she said "Tell me about Conan Doyle" because I had started telling her that part about my essay which she was going to flunk no matter what.

This was December 1965. She has a '56 Buick sedan and she said she wanted me to show her the mounds, be The Navigator and show her the mounds.

We were at the Seventh Mound and walking on the Spanish Hoofprints which she said she didn't see and asked me if I thought anybody else except Semi Senor and Mrs. Kabotie ever really saw. I couldn't believe I was driving and walking around with Mrs. Bettersen. What was I going to say? Her seats had hard wooden bead seatcovers like a person would have who never drove far. Her shoes had hard wooden soles and the toes were cut open.

Mr. Doyle who wrote fiction stories everybody believed liked photography and he just couldn't let it go that there was Spirit Photography where you could see in the picture the person's spirit. He traveled all over the world to shoot spirit pictures. This was in the 1880s or 1890s and he had a spooky album he called The Spirit Album[5] in which you could see a woman on a mule and in half of the mule's face if you looked close was rain hitting a window and it looked like a mule's woman spirit or a woman's mule spirit. Or maybe a woman was in a plain dress and in the fabric you could see fire spreading out and it was in the shape of the woman's mother's mother. Faces floated in the bright places on the photographs. People's second natures stood just behind them or next to them.

Certain people said it was the defects on what was called The Emulsion. Mr. Doyle said not but it made him a little sore if he got called a nut so about the time of The Canned Food Time in New Mexico he came here because Edgar Amos Poe and Augusto Rodin and Nathaniel Hawthorne and Herman Melvile and Walter

Whitman who were famous almost everywhere but in New Mexico said it was the place to go. They had never been here.[6]

You needed lots of sun to take photographs so Mr. Doyle came to the Mesilla Valley and he stayed at the home of General and Mrs. McKinney and he went into the sun with his camera looking for what everybody said was not there.

When it was named daguerreotype photography was called "writing with light"[7] and a lot of people didn't believe it could really be true because let's say I was writing with light now. You would say Of course you are Chum go right ahead. Sure.

Other people believed. They were right it turns out. This is what one lady named E. Barrett which is spelled the same as Victoria who's in our class wrote to somebody:

> Think of a man sitting down in the sun and leaving his facsimile in all its full completion of outline and shadow, steadfast on a plate, at the end of a minute and a half! The Mesmeric disembodiment of spirits strikes one as a degree less marvelous. And several of these wonderful portraits . . . like engraving—only exquisite and delicate beyond the work of graver—have I seen lately—longing to have such a memorial of every Being dear to me in the world. It is not merely the likeness which is precious in such cases but the association, and the sense of nearness involved in the thing . . . the fact of the very shadow of the person lying there fixed for ever! It is the very sanctification of portraits I think— and it is not at all monstrous in me to say . . . that I would rather have such a memorial of one I dearly loved, than the noblest Artist's work ever produced. I do not say so in respect (or disrespect) to Art, but for Love's sake.[8]

This was after E. Barrett's brother died that she wrote this and I found it in <u>Eternal Eye</u> by Nacho Armandine Lucie-Aurore Dupin-Lee Dudevant.

If Mr. Doyle knew E. Barrett he didn't tell. He ate canned goods here in New Mexico and he was never the same after that but he wrote five times the number of books he would have if he never took his spoons back to England with him.

"You read a great deal don't you?"

Mrs. Bettersen said that. The Seventh Mound made her sad. We were sitting in her car again. She smokes but she doesn't roll down the windows which have got smoke emulsion on them.

I told her reading was my favorite thing after Daniel died. I can go adventuring when I read.

I told her I knew whose jacket that was, that it was Daniel's and Marty's dad's jacket.

She said "Reversible."

I said that they traded it off. Marty liked the leather out and Daniel liked it in.

She said "You loved them."

She said "You loved them."

She said "You loved them."

I wasn't answering her.

She said "Tell your stepmother and the others it's okay now to stop looking for Marty."

When we were driving away from the mound she said "Tell me what Mr. Doyle did exactly."

Society

Mr. Conan Doyle took pictures of the slave descendants up and down the valley. He had a camera called a Kodak and to tell the truth it didn't use tin plates. Mr. Doyle had an assistant named Bret Harte who used a ruby lamp and chemicals and called himself The Developer but had problems because of the heat which comes right along with all that sun. They needed more Developers so they signed up people for their Society for the Study of Supernormal Pictures. The canned food poisoning was pretty awful then and people who were not in their right minds signed up.

If everything went right or everything went wrong a spirit was always in the picture of a slave descendant. The Society members wrote it all down in The Spirit Album Compendium and their note-books are somewhere in England so you can find the notebooks if you want. You can't find The Spirit Album or any of the pictures. They're gone and Sherlock Holmes himself wouldn't know how to find them I don't think.

Mrs. Bettersen said "Your sources are unreliable Mr. Belter."

No lie I said—meaning No lie Mrs. Bettersen this is the truth every part of it I could find and some parts I couldn't.

But Mrs. Bettersen thought I meant my sources were bad. She drove us slow in her car past Bridle Path and past Dip and there was her cigarette smoke you had to fan away that circled back at you. She looked in the rearview mirror which was smoky golden and she looked at the side mirrors through the emulsion windows on her side and over on mine. She wasn't paying any attention to the road. It seemed like her cigarettes burned down slower than they would have if she didn't drive so slow. She was trying to get one last look at the Seventh Mound.

You're off the road I said when we were about straddling the shoulder.

What happened next was that Mr. Doyle and Mr. Harte got pretty sick from the chemicals and the canned goods and spoons and Mr. Harte quit then to travel around and he wrote books about

163

the West that were awful lies everybody believed and that includes the people in the West.[9]

Mr. Doyle was a canned food addict like you couldn't believe and he moved back to England with just his cameras and The Compendium. He spent way too much time under the ruby lamps with his spoons and canned goods and the rest of it there in England. He wrote books too. Anybody can write books and pretty good ones. I've read a lot of them and I can tell.

Higher Places

We were way far away from statehood. We were too close to
Texas.

I told Mrs. Bettersen about the ex-votos that Mr. Rush Bradbridger showed me because I wanted to put them in here. There's
three I have put in here and there was more I could have. But I
couldn't fit the words in so there's only the pictures.

For a long time people were making the ex-votos which were
some kind of a retablo which was an offering but nothing like
a baseball card. They believed in miracles is the thing. And if a
miracle happened to you you found something you could paint
the miracle on and you wrote on it what the miracle was. My
stepmother says that the ones I put in look like they were done
on somebody's linoleum tiles that have been missing from the
floor of her pantry. The clay tiles they used in The Canned Food
Times were a lot like the linoleum of today. Sometimes you paid
somebody else to do the painting and such. Then you left it at
the altar around where all the candles were in a church. Votive
candles. Sometimes one of the ex-votos would catch on fire and
burn up and you got a negative of the picture on the plate which
before Mr. Doyle came seemed like something only God could do.

I told Mrs. Bettersen that one time Daniel found out about her
real first name. Therése. We made up a whole story about her and
Mr. Alvarezo who sure had it bad for somebody named Therése. I
asked if that was her.

It was her. My stepmother says if you want to tell the truth keep
it to three words. An angel appeared. Your breath stinks. That's bull
crap. Like that.

Anyway in The Canned Food Times people believed in miracles
more than ever and that was the time of Mr. Doyle and the Kodak.
So then people in the Mesilla Valley who couldn't buy Kodaks started
making pictures a lot more like life[10] and they hammered out their
cans and painted their miracles on the tin or on the linoleumlike
clay which made what they painted look like daguerreotype at
least a little. And what they mostly painted were miracles which

are mysteries really and Mr. Doyle learned a lot about writing his Sherlock stories from seeing all those ex-votos.

My point is something about how after awhile in History you can see how people get what they need even when they don't get what they deserve.

"Like love" said Mrs. Bettersen.

"Like love" said Mrs. Bettersen.

I heard her. She thinks I don't hear her sometimes.

I've put in here the one that is The Miracle of the Red Felt Hat. And the one that is The Miracle of the Fire Goats. And The Miracle of the Missing Guitarron. And they are in color. My dad took me downtown to the Xerox machine in Finch's Business & Office and what you get is black and white pictures of color pictures which is okay in a paper I hope. Mr. Rush Bradberger lent me the ex-votos and they are from his private collection and he took them back after I used them.

She said she came all the way from Illinois to teach in the Mesilla Valley because of Mr. Alvarezo. She was in love.

"I loved him." Three words.

Mrs. Bettersen said after Mr. Alvarezo after he got Religion real bad she stayed in the Mesilla Valley because of her students. She loved them. And there was especially Daniel's dad's children Marty and Daniel who she loved. And then Daniel's dad. "He loved me." She didn't say she loved him or not. And after she stopped loving him she loved Marty and Daniel a lot more and they needed her more. And because of Marty she loved the Mesilla Valley because Marty thought every chile field and irrigation ditch and million year old onion field was some kind of miracle. She loved Marty more and more she said. She said that you can fall in love from higher and higher places before you fall from high enough that you don't stop falling. It was like that with Marty she said. Like she was my own child she said.

The Story Complete

Porfiria Yañez McKinney, a widow, poor and her family starving, requested intercession from Señor San Francisco de Paula. On August 11, 1892, the juniper trees in Bosque Assisi near them burned from lightning. Porfiria and her eleven children watched when thirteen wild goats ran to them from the trees. One goat was on fire. He laid down in front of them. He burned quietly and long and of him they ate. The other goats permitted themselves to be fenced in order to provide for this family. Each child being given one goat, the children together raised a great herd. On this day, August 11, 1924, the funeral day of Porfiria Yañez McKinney, her family remembers this miracle granted to them.[11]

I knew Mrs. Bettersen knew. I'm going to tell it complete and omiscient because Mrs. Bettersen which is you is going to just say I'm lying anyway.

Mrs. Bettersen said when my dad told Daniel's dad that he knew what was going on and that he better stop that was when Marty disappeared and when Daniel died.

You have to understand that you can tell everything about The Canned Food Times and The Rose Mounds and Mr. Doyle and there's more to tell. You can try but you never run out of History. After you run out of Faith you have got History which people put their Faith in who are not religious at all.

I loved Daniel I said.

I loved him I said.

After everything after Daniel died and nobody could find Marty that's when Mrs. Bettersen went out. She knew where Marty was hiding. She went to her. Bus the bus driver was hiding her on his bus.

She put that jacket on me. The red part with the brown leather ribbing was inside. We were quiet a whole lot a long time falling and falling and you remember that and I know you do Mrs. Bettersen no matter what you say or what grade you give me.

167

I'm not Marty I told Mrs. Bettersen.

I'm not Daniel I said.

But she looked at me from a high place real high real close. No lie.

Señor de la Miseracordia granted to D. Magdalena
Ray Man Celaya that her son Tomás should have no
more head pain. A red hat, very large, made from
good felt, was revealed to Tomás in the ocotillo fence
on February 3, 1903. The hat fit tight, its band crush-
ing pain. It cooled his head and hid his eyes from sun
stabbing them. To drink water from it healed fear. This
when the name of el Señor de la Miseracordia was in-
voked. In recompense Grandfather Ray Man dedicates
to him this retablo.[12]

She had to kill Daniel's dad. She had to know that Marty would
be okay. So she killed him pretty easy with a pillow. She thought
maybe he wanted to die because it went pretty easy she said. He
fell asleep. He slept forever.

After she took Marty into Mexico the next day right off she
came back to Las Almas. And drove around in her Buick. And
there it was.

The Seventh Mound was a good place to bury him.

And she and Madame Edna Zaldivar Kabotie have kept up a
chess game making people ask where the child is instead of where
is Daniel's dad. Everybody thought he just ran away somewhere.

Mrs. Bettersen and Madame Kabotie paid for Marty to be okay
in a boatmaking village in Mexico where she can grow up and see
Mrs. Bettersen all the time. They make lifeboats in that village for
all the big ships in the world and for the ships with rafts too because for people to feel safe you need to see lifeboats.

How? I asked.

"I visit her" she said. "All the time."

I wanted to know something else. How do you hide Daniel's dad's
body and get it to the mound and bury it and no one knows.

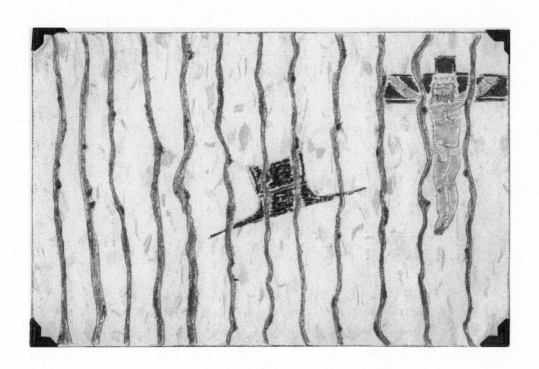

On March 26, The Feast of the Annunciation of Our
Lord, in the year of 1901, Ambrosio Lapid Arbuso
found his guitarron lost for many sad months. It was
filled with stones and put at the bottom of a shallow
pond. The Santo Niño de Lagos found this guitarron
by making geese pluck its strings under the water.
The music brought rescuers. Ambrosio plays again for
money and for the fiestas, he forgives his enemy, the
guitarron having a tone now as of rising bubbles, and
he makes this offering in praise.[13]

It's only the men who didn't know she said and said "Madame
Kabotie knows. Bet knows. Other women. Mrs. Orofolo. Mrs.
Burhart. They helped me."

When I said she was a liar she said "How do you know Mr.
Belter?" She asked me if I would like to keep the jacket which I
would and she doesn't really know how much I would. Whenever
I wear it it reminds me that it proves nothing. But I like to have
something that is Daniel's. I like that.

FOOTNOTES

[1]Gregory Nazianzen <u>Armorers</u> pgs. 1–4.

[2]H. Immel Heber <u>The Human System Volume I</u> pg. 3081.

[3]Fabian Lasuen <u>On the Can</u> pg. 27.

[4]Isidore H.W. Ferrer <u>Spam: A Passion</u> pgs. 1–55.

[5]Sir Arthur Conan Doyle "The Combermere Photograph" <u>Quarterly Transactions of the British College of Psychic Science 5 October 1926</u> pgs. 190–192.

[6]Una Hawthorne <u>New Mexico: Land of Likenesses</u> pg. iii.

[7]Beatricia Lavender-Evan <u>Plumbe's Gallery</u> pgs. 2–303.

[8]Betty Miller Ed. <u>Elizabeth Barrett to Miss Mitford: The Unpublished Letters of Elizabeth Barrett to Mary Russell Mitford</u> pgs. 208–209.

[9]Stephen Vicar <u>All Harte</u> pg. vi.

[10]Bunnie Goldensmyth <u>Canned Realism</u> pgs. 87.

[11]Owned by Mr. Rush Bradbridger

[12]Owned by Mr. Rush Bradbridger.

[13]Owned by Mr. Rush Bradbridger.

BIBLIOGRAPHY

Rush Bradbridger. Owner <u>The Miracle of the Fire Goats</u> 1965.

Rush Bradbridger. Owner <u>The Miracle of the Missing Guitarron</u> 1965.

Rush Bradbridger. Owner <u>The Miracle of the Red Felt Hat</u> 1965.

Sir Arthur Conan Doyle. "The Combermere Photograph" <u>Quarterly Transactions of the British College of Psychic Science</u> 5 October 1926.

Isidore H.W. Ferrer. <u>Spam: A Passion</u>. Pius X New Mexico: Hookseam Press 1956.

Bunnie Goldensmyth. <u>Canned Realism</u>. Boston: Dominican Editions 1963.

Bret Harte. <u>The Luck of Roaring Camp and Other Sketches</u>. London: Hamlin & Harrison 1870.

Bret Harte. <u>Tales of the Argonauts</u>. London: Hamlin & Harrison 1875.

Una Hawthorne. <u>New Mexico: Land of Likenesses</u>. Knot: New Mexico: Burnham Books 1950.

H. Immel Heber. <u>The Human Spirit Volume I</u>. Juarez: Ribera Ediciones 1946.

Fabian Lasuen. <u>On the Can</u>. Dixon: JMJ and Co. 1954.

Beatricia Lavender-Evan. <u>Plumbe's Gallery</u>. Jerome Arizona: Sigmaringen Bible College Imprints 1939.

Betty Miller Ed. <u>Elizabeth Barrett to Miss Mitford: The Unpublished Letters of Elizabeth Barrett to Mary Russell Mitford</u>. London: John Murray 1965.

Gregory Nazianzen. <u>Armorers</u>. Dallas: Lewis Carroll College 1960.

Stephen Vicar. <u>All Harte</u>. Narcissus New York: Georgewillows and Co. 1953.

Kevin McIlvoy teaches in the Department of English at New Mexico State University, and in the MFA Program for Writers at Warren Wilson College. Recently, he has taught at the Bread Loaf, RopeWalk, and Arizona State University writers' conferences. He has been the editor in chief of *Puerto del Sol,* the NMSU national literary magazine, for twenty-three years, and has published his own work in literary magazines, including *TriQuarterly,* the *Southern Review, River City, Ploughshares,* and the *Missouri Review. The Complete History of New Mexico* is his first story collection; he has published four novels, *A Waltz, The Fifth Station, Little Peg,* and *Hyssop.* He and his family live in Las Cruces, New Mexico.

Acknowledgments

For inspiration, guidance, and patient supportiveness,
I thank Margee McIlvoy, Fiona McCrae, Katie Dublinski,
Janna Rademacher, J. Robbins, Anne Czarniecki, Tony Hoagland,
Ellen Bryant Voigt, Miriam Altshuler, Pete Turchi,
Bruce & Mary Streett, Leora Zeitlin, Nat Sobel, Bernadette Smyth,
Rick Russo, Ann Rohovec, Rita Popp, Beth O'Leary,
Antonya Nelson, Paula Moore, Deborah LaPorte,
Kent Jacobs & Sallie Ritter, Chris Hale, Reg Gibbons, Jim Earley,
Michael Collier, Chris Burnham, Robert Boswell, Charles Baxter,
Andrea Barrett, Sara McGhee, Bobby & Lee Byrd and family,
the Outlaws, and Terry Stright of Elk Mountain Lodge.

The text of the short stories is set in Méridien,
a typeface designed in 1954 by Adrian Frutiger.
The text of the title story, "The Complete History
of New Mexico," is set in American Typewriter, a typeface
designed in 1974 by Joel Kaden and Tony Stan.

Book design by Wendy Holdman.
Manufactured by Friesens on acid-free paper.